Gertrude Douglas

Brown as a Berry

Vol. 1

Gertrude Douglas

Brown as a Berry
Vol. 1

ISBN/EAN: 9783337349172

Printed in Europe, USA, Canada, Australia, Japan

Cover: Foto ©Andreas Hilbeck / pixelio.de

More available books at **www.hansebooks.com**

BROWN AS A BERRY.

A Novel.

BY

GEORGE DOUGLAS.

"That piebald mixture of black and white, called Man."

IN THREE VOLUMES.

VOL. I.

LONDON:

TINSLEY BROTHERS, 8, CATHERINE STREET, STRAND.

1874.

LONDON:

SAVILL, EDWARDS AND CO., PRINTERS, CHANDOS STREET,
COVENT GARDEN.

TO

THE RIGHT HONOURABLE THE EARL OF HOME

THIS STORY,

WITH HIS 'LORDSHIP'S KIND PERMISSION,

Is respectfully Dedicated

BY HIS MOST OBEDIENT AND FAITHFUL SERVANT,

THE AUTHOR.

BROWN AS A BERRY.

PROLOGUE.

Scene I.

ABOUT eight o'clock on a bright frosty morning in December, 185—, a boy called Luke Mark—who was spending his Christmas holidays at the home of Jack Ferrier, his friend and schoolmate—was walking through the shrubbery of Blackbeck House. He is rather a nice-looking lad, with fair complexion, blue eyes, and hair of a shade a little darker than pale flaxen, and is fifteen years of age.

In his hand he carries a catapult, from which he occasionally projects a stone with considerable force.

Scratching about among the dead leaves and withered stalks of last summer's flowers in the shrubbery, are some poultry. There is a cock and five hens. They are of a kind particularly prized by the owner of Blackbeck House, who has recently been assigned a gold cup for their excellence at a show held in the neighbouring town of Marchton some weeks before.

Without thinking what he is doing, and as much out of idleness as mischief, Mark picks up a stone, fixes it in his catapult, and taking aim, hits one of the five hens on the head, which drops down dead. Pleased with his success, and unaware or forgetful that these are the prize poultry, he takes another stone and fires it, and after that another, until the cock and the five hens are all killed.

It is not until he sees the unfortunate poultry lying prostrate on the ground that the thoughtless and mischievous boy awakens to the full perception of the consequences of his action. If the birds had been of a common breed he could easily have repaired the damage by purchasing some new fowls with his pocket money, but these particular ones had been sent to Mr. Ferrier from abroad, and were, he firmly believed, the only specimens of the sort in England.

"By George! I've done it now!" exclaims Mark, contemplating the dead poultry with unutterable horror, and dropping the catapult as though it had stung him or burnt his fingers, he tries to get the cock on its legs, but of course without success. "The beggar is as dead as mutton!"

Then he reflects that being a visitor at Blackbeck House, it is not probable that Mr. Ferrier will do more than look glum or give a severe reprimand. He is duly thankful he is not one of Mr. Ferrier's own sons, or he knows, in schoolboy phrase, "he would catch it like mad."

While thus thinking, two boys appear at the corner of the house with skates slung over their arms. These are Mr. Ferrier's two sons, William and Jack. The former is the same age as Luke Mark; the other three years younger.

"Come on, Luke," shouts Jack. "I've been down to the big pond, and it's bearing all over. We need not come home until five o'clock, as we're to dine with the rest to-night. And mother's given me lots of grub, and a shilling besides to buy some pale ale."

"No, really? How stunning!" returns Mark, and without another thought about the unlucky poultry, he scampers off with the rest of the boys. Something is sure to turn up between this and the evening. He does just once wish, but it is merely a passing wish in the excitement of a stirring game of hockey, that he had had the sense to dig a hole and bury the poultry, and then it might have been supposed they had been stolen.   However, it is too late now for any regrets to be of use.

The three boys have scarcely got out of sight, when Mr. Ferrier, with a cigar in his mouth, walks through the shrubbery on his way to the stables.

Almost the first thing which meets his eye is the catapult beside the dead bodies of the defunct cock and hens.   The next minute he has called all the servants out of the house, and is questioning them very minutely as to the author of the deed—on which subject, however, no one is able to throw any light.   Mr. Ferrier then lifts up the catapult, on which is written distinctly the initials J. F.

" J. F.   That stands for Jack Ferrier," he says.   " I think I have discovered who killed my poor prize poultry, and I shall give him something to-night which will make him leave off these practical jokes."

The servants go back to the house, congratulating themselves they are not Master Jack. After this, Mr. Ferrier cuts several tough branches from an old ash tree at the end of the shrubbery, and as he *swishes* them one after the other through the air, regrets there will not be time to season them properly ; but, nevertheless, they will answer the purpose for which he intends them. Then Mr. Ferrier rides over to Marchton, where he has a business engagement which occupies him for the remainder of the day.

Towards evening the boys return, very hungry and rosy from their long skate. Dinner not being quite ready, they employ themselves in making toffy over a blazing fire in the library. Charity Ferrier, a pretty graceful girl of fourteen, already admired in Marchton, is sitting with the boys. She has a great love of ruling, and tyrannizes over her mother—a gentle woman, idolized by her husband and sons.

"How my chilblains rage!" exclaims Jack, rubbing his right hand, on the palm of which a large chilblain has thought fit to settle. "Hark! that's the sound of the carriage taking mother off to the Towers. She's going to dine there to-night."

"There's some one coming along the passage," says Charity, as a heavy tread is heard outside the door.

Mark gives a start.

Has Mr. Ferrier found out who did it? He remembers he never thought of looking whether any one had been standing at the window. Until this moment he had completely forgotten the disagreeable fact. His heart and his courage seem slipping right into the heels of his shoes, as Mr. Ferrier enters the room.

He is a tall, powerfully-built man, with a stern cast of features which can look very severe when angry, and just now he is very angry.

But for the light of the fire burning clear and brilliant in the frost, it is dusk in the library. The leaping flames throw the figures of the slim girl and her flaxen curls, and the three expectant boys, into dark Rembrandt shadows and warm softened lights, touching the countenances with the mellow tints produced by holding a candle at a little distance in a darkened room.

There has been a splendid sunset over the broad expanse of the flat Lincolnshire fens, the creeks, and morasses, and quicksands of its dangerous coast, and the sun itself has sunk behind the wolds, leaving some ragged crimson clouds floating over the burnished orange-gold sky, against which stand out some tall, straight, weird poplar-trees, and the steeple of Marchton church.

"Do any of you boys here know who killed my prize poultry?" begins Mr. Ferrier.

"No, sir," return the three boys at once— two of them with perfect truth; the other a little hesitatingly. But after all Luke argues, *did* he do it? What fools the birds were to get in his way; and to be sure, it was the *stone* which finished the poultry, not he.

"I asked you," proceeds Mr. Ferrier, "to give Jack a chance of acknowledging the wanton mischief he has done. I shall not take the trouble of contradicting you. Stand forward, Jack. Do you recognise this catapult?"

"Yes, it's mine," replies Jack.

"Where do you think I found it? Lying beside the dead poultry."

"I did not kill them, father," protests the boy; "I know nothing about it."

"Was it you, William?"

"No, sir."

"Was it you, Luke Mark?"

"No, sir."

Luke detests himself for the lie. But he sees those ground-ashes in Mr. Ferrier's hand, and he has felt them on his back before now, and did not like the application. Now that he has denied it, the confession would be all the more difficult.

"Have any of you had Jack's catapult?" goes on Mr. Ferrier. "Some of you may have taken it by mistake."

But William steadfastly denies having done so, and Mark corroborates him.

"Then, my man, you had better confess at once," says Mr. Ferrier. "I shall give you a thrashing as you deserve, but it wont be so bad as if you stick to your lie."

" I didn't do it," is all Jack answers.

Mark feels what a coward he is as the ash falls with a swinging whizz on Jack's back, yet fond as he is of his chum and school friend, he cannot compel his courage to return sufficiently to save the boy from the punishment which is justly his own.

When three ground-ashes are broken to bits, and some rents are visible on Jack's jacket, Mr. Ferrier pauses to take a fresh one. Jack has hitherto been silent.

" Will you confess now ?" he asks.

" No, I wont," he replies. " I've nothing to confess."

Mr. Ferrier is thoroughly enraged at what he considers Jack's stubbornness and obstinacy. Brought up himself on the principle of " Spare the rod, spoil the child," he has no notion of letting Jack off one inch of what he thinks proper correction. He has no idea of condoning an offence. If a man or boy has sinned or offended, he deserves punishment. He believes that the old-fashioned system produces finer and more honourable men than the present style—men, in fact, capable of heroism and of uncomplaining endurance.

"Hold out your hand, Jack," he commands.

Jack extends the left, hoping his father will not ask for the right.

"Not that one," cries Mr. Ferrier, exasperated beyond measure at his son, and snatching the boy's right hand, he proceeds to rain blow after blow upon the palm on which is the chilblain before mentioned. Jack sets his teeth hard; but do what he will he cannot prevent a low cry of intense pain escaping his lips; for every blow of the ash causes exquisite torture in the inflamed flesh, and each stroke draws blood.

Mark cannot stand it any longer, and catches hold of the ground-ash, crying out—

"Oh, Mr. Ferrier, please don't; he did not do it."

Jack looks gratefully at his champion, but holds his tongue.

"It's very good of you, Mark," says Mr. Ferrier; "but if Jack did not do it, who did?"

Much as Mark loves Jack, he is unable to avow the truth. No one could hate his cowardice more than he does himself, still he cannot bring himself to speak out.

"Will you confess now?" again says Mr. Ferrier.

Jack only shakes his head. He has nearly

bitten his nether lip through, in the effort to restrain his cries.

"Well, you've about had enough for to-day," observes Mr. Ferrier. "It'll take you a little while to get over this; perhaps by that time you'll have come to your senses. I'm determined to break you of these mischievous tricks. I wish you would take pattern of your friend Mark; he is all that a gentleman should be, quiet, polite, and still not a muff."

Calling Charity to come to dinner with William and Mark, he leaves Jack alone, after telling him he is to have neither dinner nor supper that day.

Jack has, indeed, "about had enough." He sits down on the rug and wraps his bleeding hand in his pocket-handkerchief, feeling very dizzy and "queer;" then, overpowered by the heat of the fire, the pain in his back, and the agony of his wounded member, he faints off quietly on to the floor.

"Coom, coom, Measter Ja-ack," says a voice, when all have gone in to dinner, which, had Jack been conscious, he would have recognised as that of the fat cook. His misfortunes have spread to the kitchen, and the worthy head of the culinary regions, with whom, in spite of many tricks, he has always been first favourite, has brought him some food. " Doan't ee be stünt, Measter Ja-ack. Coom, coom now," as if addressing a refractory horse. " Hoowiver, I've fetched ee some maazin' foin fried taates, and if ee dosen't eat 'em I'll eat un mysen." Then fancying she hears Mr. Ferrier leaving the dining-room, she shuffles off to her own domain. No one comes to Jack. Mr. Ferrier insists that Charity and the boys shall remain in the drawing-room, and as he is completely master in his own house, his will is implicitly observed. Mark is excessively uncomfortable at the notice paid him by Mr. Ferrier. He begged to be allowed to take Jack some dinner; but was peremptorily refused. The praise lavished on him of generosity, hurts him almost as much as the ground-ashes did Jack's back. What evil spirit induced him to shy stones at the poultry? He has relinquished any feeble intention he might have had of telling now. Jack will soon be all right again, and he will endeavour to compensate him in some way for the severe thrashing he has had.

The moon has risen high in the sky, and the stars are shining over the wolds, a dark undulating ridge against the horizon, and the shadows of the leafless trees are cast black on the dry, hard ground, when some one with a lamp in her hand enters the library.

Jack has come to himself sometime ago, but was too stiff and cold to care to move. So he lay still where he was. He opens his eyes to see a woman in white satin, with diamonds gleaming in the smooth folds of her dark, braided hair, bending over him. For the moment, he imagines he beholds some beautiful creation of dreamland—not a real woman in flesh and blood. And years afterwards, when in the wilds of California and the gay city of San Francisco, in the depths of an American pine forest, and up the banks of the Yang-t'se-Kiang, he remembers how fair his mother looked in the radiance of the moonlight. They are very like each other—this mother and son—only Jack is the plain edition of a charming woman. Both have black hair and steel-grey eyes, with black lashes and black brows; but Mrs. Ferrier's mouth and nose are well formed, while Jack's are nothing out of the ordinary.

"My dear boy," she says, placing her arms tenderly round him, "you have been in trouble, I hear. Why did not you admit you had done it, if you had?"

"I wasn't going to say I'd done it when I

hadn't.   I wouldn't to escape a worse thrashing than I had to-night," replies the boy, sturdily and somewhat sulkily.

" You did not do it then, Jack?"

" No, mother, I didn't."

Mrs. Ferrier stoops down and kisses her youngest child, the apple of her eye, her daily anxiety.

" Father does *rile* a fellow so; he never believes one, even upon one's oath.   And then he keeps saying he must ' *break*' one in.   I'd die sooner than be *broken in.*"

" Jack, Jack! he says you were sulky, but I think he was mistaken.   You know he valued the poultry greatly, and it is very annoying that they should have been killed.   It was natural he was angry.   But, my dear boy, what is the matter with your jacket?   Have you torn it?"

" No," says Jack, " it's the ground-ashes that did it.   But it's an *old jacket*, so it's no matter."

" You must be terribly hurt," she exclaims, turning the lamp so as to throw light on his back.   " Why, your jacket and shirt are slit to bits!   Surely your father——" she stops, for to preserve peace and harmony between father and son is the object of her life, and young as he is,

Jack has a keen sense of justice. He believes his father has a pleasure in singling him out as an offender on all occasions.   Mrs. Ferrier is anxious to remove this unfortunate feeling, but this event will not tend to improve their relations.

"My back will be all serene in a couple of weeks. I daresay it is black and blue. It's my hand that hurts most," pulling it out from his trousers'-pocket. The handkerchief had dried into the wound, and an attempt to drag it off produced a flow of blood. "Take care of your pretty gown, mother. It'll make no end of a mess of it," he cries, anxiously.

" Oh, never mind the gown," she says, " you had better go to bed now, and I'll try and doctor up this poor hand."

Mark is sleeping in Jack's room; but his qualms of conscience keep him still awake. He is a warm-hearted boy, sincerely attached to Jack, and considerably spoilt by the uncle and aunt who, in the absence of either father or mother, have brought him up. He shams being asleep, however, while Mrs. Ferrier, after pinning her white satin gown out of her way, bathes Jack's hand with warm water, and is thus enabled to remove the dried stiffened handkerchief. He hears Mrs. Ferrier wonder why Jack did not say he had not been in the shrubbery that morning, as William could have proved he was with him at the pond; and listens to Jack's reply, it would have been useless, Mr. Ferrier having determined beforehand he was guilty.

"Are you warmer now?" asks Mrs. Ferrier.

"Yes, this jolly hot stuff has warmed me to the ends of my feet. Give Luke there a wineglass of it. He tried to beg me off, you know."

Luke is compelled to sit up and partake of the negus, and it is doubtful if any coals of fire ever felt hotter, or if any act of Jack's could have gone further towards knitting together and cementing firmer his respect and friendship for his chum.

"You are very kind, Mrs. Ferrier," he stammers.

"I am fond of boys, especially of school boys," smiles the pretty woman, who shines as much at home as in society. She does not wish to "mollycoddle" her sons, and trusts they will grow up brave, fearless, truth-speaking men, but she resolves Jack shall never again be so severely punished as he has been this evening. Such a little lad, too, she thinks, as she looks at the dark head reposing on the white pillow. How could Mr. Ferrier have done it? It was a pity he should be so fatally convinced that Jack of necessity must always do wrong, and never right.

"Mother, you're a *trump!*" says Jack suddenly, pulling her face down to him by the uninjured hand, and giving her a hearty kiss.

Then Mrs. Ferrier whispers something.

"I weant, I weant," he answers, in broad Lincolnshire, "I'll *niver* forgive 'un."

"Yes, you will, dear."

"Well," very reluctantly, "for *you* I will."

Mark lies awake for some time after Mrs. Ferrier has gone. What a nasty little sneak I have been, he reflects. But if it were to come over again, he knows he would just do the same. Now that the room is dark and the whole house hushed and quiet, he thinks he might unburden his conscience. Now or never.

"Jack," he calls, "Jack—I say, Jack." But the only answer is a prolonged and prosaic *snore*. So, having done his duty, and relieved his mind by attempting to tell, he turns over on his side and goes to sleep.

Scene II.

It is six years since Mr. Ferrier was enraged by the mysterious death of his prize poultry. This still remains unexplained, and probably will continue to do so. However, it has long ago been forgotten.

The family party, consisting of Mr. and Mrs. Ferrier, Charity, William, and Jack, are in the library, where Jack had been thrashed that winter evening for what he had never done.

Now it is summer time.

Mr. Ferrier is speaking.

"You may do as you like, Jack, but you are a fool if you refuse. It is eight hundred a year, even if you clap in a curate and pay him a hundred. You need only preach one sermon in the year. That's what old Burnley did. Preached one sermon in the twelve months, drove to church in his carriage, brought his own port with him—easy as A B C."

"I don't think I'm fitted for the Church," replies Jack, quietly. He is a tall well-made youth, rather in the hobbledehoy stage as yet, but giving promise of being, though not hand-some, a manly-looking fellow. " Besides, I should not like to put in a curate to do all the hard work and give him only a hundred a year, while I did nothing and was paid eight hundred. It doesn't seem fair."

" You are very silly, Jack," says Charity. She has grown into an elegant woman, and is now engaged to a Lieutenant Napier, who has excellent prospects from a wealthy great-uncle, who has already reached the age of threescore years and ten.

" What would you advise me to do, mother ?" asks Jack.

" What you think right and honourable," re-joins Mrs. Ferrier. " I should like much the best to have you settled near us; but if it is against your inclinations, I had rather you did not."

" You'll never have such an opportunity again," pursues Mr. Ferrier. " And think of the position you would have. A clergyman can move in the best society, and——"

" You might be a bishop, and be called my lord," suggests Charity.

" As well say an archbishop at once," laughs Jack. " Oh yes; and I'd have you all over to stay with me three months in the year at the

Archiepiscopal Palace. 'How does that sound for high,' as a Yankee chap I met the other day said?"

"Your figure is just suited for the style of dress, knee-breeches and all that," says William.

"I am not cut out for a parson," returns Jack. "Why, when I stood up in the pulpit to preach and saw the congregation sitting before me, I should be in such a blue funk, I'd want to hook out into the vestry. I shouldn't be a bit happier for being called my lord. In fact, it would make me very uncomfortable. It requires a special vocation to become a clergyman, and I haven't got any vocation. You would be having serious complaints that the Rev. J. Ferrier attended coursing matches and steeple-chases; that he hunted in pink in Lent—I shouldn't be able to help it, if I'd a good horse, and there happened to be a meet with the scent lying well — or that he drove tandem to church."

"Vocation be hanged!" breaks in Mr. Ferrier. "You don't want a vocation. Any one can be a clergyman. You've only to get up a certain tone in reading; and as to preaching the sermons, you can buy a lot ready to hand, and you can copy them out on Saturday night in clear writing."

"I am very much obliged to Mr. Tresham for the offer, but I must decline it," says Jack.

"Then you are a born fool, and I shall wash my hands of you altogether," replies Mr. Ferrier, angrily. "Now, Alice, don't back him up in his folly."

"It isn't that I *wont* : it's because I *can't*, mother," responds Jack, looking appealingly at Mrs. Ferrier.

"Well, Jack, if you wont accept it, I'll tell you what I shall do. I shall pay your outfit to Shanghai, and your journey money, and give you three hundred pounds to keep yourself until you find something to do. I daresay Luke Mark will give you some help. You understand that is your portion. I can't afford a penny more, so it will be useless your attempting to ask me. If it is not enough, you must go without."

"Oh, John; it's such a distance across the sea to China," pleads Mrs. Ferrier.

"Now, Jack," says her husband, in a more conciliatory tone, "if you go away, you'll break your mother's heart, and it will be the fault of your obduracy. Somehow or another she is awfully attached to you, young scamp as you are. Don't you see it would be better for yourself and for all of us if you would agree to be a clergyman and settle at Marshley close beside us? You could do all those things you spoke of in moderation. Muscular Christianity is the order of the day."

"If mother really wants me, and thinks I ought, I'll try to enter the Church; but I know I was never made for a parson. One ought to have better motives than a good settlement in life, good society, and good position— and honestly those would be mine."

"Then I think Jack had better not force himself," replies Mrs. Ferrier. "If any good is to come of it, I thoroughly agree with him, the motives ought to be of the very highest and purest character, as it is the noblest profession on earth."

"Very well," answers Mr. Ferrier. "Then it's the three hundred pounds and China. You always spoilt that boy, Alice."

"Dear Jack! I don't know how I shall ever part with him."

"He ought to have gone into the Church, and there would have been no parting for you. Fancy a fat living of 900*l.* a year, and hardly any work to do, going a begging!"

Scene III.

It is a magnificent moonlight night in the Island of Formosa.

The air is alive with fireflies, and the long rolling waves shine with phosphoric light. The Datura trees wave their blooming masses as a night breeze passes by, and one or two perfumed spikes fall sleepily from among them to the ground. Far over the moonlit waters the silver radiance glimmers, showing a sail and the red gleam of a lamp at the head of a steamer anchored at a bend in the bay, some little distance from the shore.

Moored high and dry on the beach is a boat, and two sailors in the dress of " Green's Merchant Service " are waiting near it.

Through the tropical splendour of the glorious southern night come a man and a woman, both in the prime of life and beauty. She rides a milk-white ox, which crushes the sweet-scented waxen cinnamon flowers beneath its heavy feet. They go under arches of scarlet and purple passion flowers, among which the fireflies flit in and out ; their dancing lights flickering hither and thither like tiny globules of flame over the heads of the man and woman, as they journey downwards to the sea shore.

The man leans his hand caressingly on the arm of the woman, when they are within a few paces of the boat and the sailors, and looks up into her face.

"My Lilith !" he says, with profound tenderness in his deep tones, "mon idole! mon âme !"

"Will you be faithful after what I have abandoned for you ?" she asks. "I have forsaken all to follow you."

CHAPTER I.

"GOOD morning, Mum; I hope you haf brought your umbrella with you. The weather here has been very wet and stormy. All the pupils have cried one after the oder. It is one great consolation to see you, for *you* never cry, Thyrza. You are as dry as von leetle sponge."

Sitting down at the piano, Thyrza Rutherfurd strikes the first notes of the Sonata pathétique. Mr. Spindler rises from his chair and paces round the room, his hands behind his back, and beats time with a long ruler. He is an elderly man, very fat and stumpy, with strongly marked aquiline features, snow white hair, and an irrepressible propensity for taking unlimited quantities of snuff. "Ach, mein Gott! A wrong note there," he cries, in a tone of unspeakable anguish. "F♯ I tell you, Mum, slower, slower; you play as if your fingers were running away with you. F♯ I say, Mum."

" There is no F♯ printed where I am playing," the girl ventures to remonstrate.

" Not dere, of course. I mean two bars previous," he responds, having looked all over the page to find a place where F♯ is marked. " That fingering will never do! Begin again from the top of the page."

Accordingly, Thyrza recommences and proceeds smoothly enough for some time; when Mr. Spindler, suddenly resuming his seat, abruptly jerks her hands from the key-board, exclaiming in a voice of thunder, " *What* are you doing, Mum ?"

Taken by surprise, and almost electrified by his unexpected attack, she springs up from the music stool, almost overturning it in her rapid movements, and cries out—

" Oh, Monsieur Spindler !"

" Well, well ! I intended not to terrify thee," says he, consolingly, taking possession of her vacated seat, and running his fingers lightly over the notes. " What wild frightened eyes thou hast ! But that *enfant terrible* who precede thee, it is one mistake that she learn music ! She make me mad, crazy, distracted. I no able to sit still when she play ! I spik' English like my own tongue, is it not so ? but she no understand, and when I tell her she is

all out of time she do nothing but cry, cry, cry,
'oh!'" shaking his head and groaning deeply.
" It is *awful!*"

As Mr. Spindler relates his troubles, the
twanging of a guitar is heard outside the open
window through which the old man sees the
sunburnt face of a ragged Italian boy. He
is dancing on the pavement to solicit alms for
himself and his guinea-pig, which small animal
he holds tucked tightly under his arm while
he turns and twists and leaps with a grace
and litheness in his supple slender limbs that
is nature's own gift.

A tattered hat adorned with some peacock's
feathers is placed on the back of his jet black
locks, beneath which shine a pair of melting
brown eyes. An orange-coloured cravat, fastened
under his chin, conceals sundry deficiencies in
the front of his not over-clean shirt, and the
guitar is slung over his shoulder by a bit of
red twine.

The street is narrow, and as each story rises
higher it approaches in proximity to its neighbours, so closely that at last the houses almost
meet in friendly touch, and only a small piece of
sky above is visible to the foot passengers below.
Opposite the *pension* in which Thyrza is having
her music lesson is the old hotel of the Flying

Dragon, whither travellers *en route* for the Rhine country occasionally resort. The gorgeous sign of the Flying Dragon, painted with bright scarlet on a golden ground, which hangs suspended over the grey weather-beaten arched entrance to the courtyard beyond, is the only morsel of colour or light in the sombre dusky *rue*.

The diligence, running for the convenience of the public between Villios and Trois d'Or, a little village ten miles distant, has just arrived. The tired dusty horses draw up, and from the inside of the vehicle descend several jaded English tourists, two Sisters of Charity with sweet gentle faces, one gentleman in a light grey overcoat and a tall handsome woman attired in the barbaric contrast of a grass green satin gown with a ruby bonnet. She has on a thick black veil, and turns her steps at once in the direction of the *pension*, formerly a convent dedicated to S. Sebastian the Martyr, but now consecrated to the education of young ladies under the fostering care of Miss Holt, a spinster of an undecided age, though of a very decided temper.

The Italian picks up some *sous* thrown to him by the gentleman, and begins again his *impromptu tarentelle* before the window of the room where Thyrza and Mr. Spindler are sitting, this time accompanying his music and dance with a song, in a clear, childish treble voice. He dances as much for the mere pleasure of being alive this fine spring morning, and for the delight in the quick motion, as for the sake of the filthy lucre he may gain.

The Sonata pathétique andante movement is out of the question.

"I go crazy!" exclaims Mr. Spindler; "it is but this moment there was ein horrible brass band to whom I give a franc not to play. Then there was a man selling flowers, and a woman with vegetables; and now this imp has come. It is too *moch*. Will you go away, sar?"

The Italian laughs, but only redoubles his exertions, singing louder and dancing faster—a picture, in his rags and dirt, for a painter. Mr. Spindler does not take this view of the case at all.

"Andate al diavolo!" he shouts, at the top of his voice, to the astonished boy, opening the window wider; and doubling his fists, he shakes them menacingly, throwing as much ferociousness into his mild blue eyes as he can impart to them.

Terrified at the irate countenance glaring forth upon him, the child drops his little guinea-pig, which scuttles across the street under the body of the diligence, appearing among the hoofs of the horses.

"Oh! my only friend!" the boy exclaims, in French, rushing after his pet. Heedless of his own safety, he crawls beneath the fresh horses the ostler is attaching to the worn-out rope harness for the return journey to Trois d'Or, and succeeds in catching the guinea-pig; but as he rises, his foot trips on the loosely-hanging string of his guitar, and he falls, striking his head against a projecting stone of the uneven pavement. There he lies motionless. The guinea-pig, with more affection than is generally supposed to be possessed by their species, walks up his breast, looking into his face as if to inquire what is the matter with his master.

Mr. Spindler, on witnessing the accident, is instantly smitten with remorse, considering himself the original cause of the misfortune.

"Vat haf I done?" he laments; "mein Gott! the leetle knabe is dead, and I haf killed him! Thyrza, run quickly—get through the window—you jomp easily down; it is but von leetle distance. Go, and I will come out by the front door. Go," seeing Thyrza hesitate, "Miss Holt will not know—she is at the other side of the house—and if she does, I will settle everything. Run."

In obedience to his orders, Thyrza lets herself drop down into the street by the window, which is only about two feet from the ground, and hastens to the assistance of the boy.

The gentleman in the light overcoat, who arrived in the diligence, has hitherto been occupied in counting over his luggage, but he abandons this employment on noticing the mishap to the small Italian, and by the time Thyrza reaches the hotel of the Flying Dragon, has lifted the child from the ground and is sitting on the pavement, holding him in his arms. The guinea-pig has taken refuge in the pocket of the boy's threadbare, tattered jacket, and peers curiously out with its round, black eyes.

"I think I will carry him into the hotel," says the gentleman, speaking apparently more for his own benefit than for that of any one in particular. Then he addresses Thyrza directly.

"Perhaps you will have the kindness to help me in rising. The boy is not a light weight."

Thyrza extends her hand. He seizes it with no very gentle grasp, and, regaining his feet, enters the doorway of the Flying Dragon. Thyrza follows at a modest distance behind him to see what the end will be. In her way she nearly stumbles headlong over a pile of luggage, addressed to J. Ferrier, Esq. A porter is

arranging the boxes in a curiously artistic manner, placing the small parcels first and the large
ones on the top of them, the result of which she
inwardly prophesies will be an immediate down-
fall.

Just opposite an open door reveals a large
fire blazing in a capacious grate, a clean sanded
floor, several rows of shining brass, copper,
and pewter pots, pans and dish-covers; cup-
boards filled with china and crockeryware ornament the darkened walls, while a pleasant smell,
as of savoury meat cooking, issues into the
passage.

Mr. Ferrier halts here a moment, then turns
in at a door on the lefthand side of the
kitchen. This room is misty with smoke, and
reeking with the fumes of tobacco. It is the
billiard-room of the hotel, where travellers, if
they wish, may also be provided with coffee and
the *petite presse* of the day.

Originally the Flying Dragon was a nobleman's house, and it still retains traces of its
former aristocratic owner in the ornaments
of carved wood which decorate the mantel-pieces
of most of the apartments. The billiard-room
is panelled with black oak, one large thick beam,
ornamented with rich carvings of pomegranates
and hop leaves, crosses transversely the low

ceiling, let in with paintings on wood of various historic scenes, executed with rather more than ordinary skill by some Flemish painter long since dead and gone. The fireplace is wide, and inlaid with encaustic tiles. Properly speaking there is no grate; an iron brazier, rusty with age and damp, in winter holds a handful of fire, but for the nonce the brazier contains a delf jug filled with spring flowers, whose scent is completely lost in the fumes of tobacco.

In this quaint room, in which one would rather fancy the gay costumes of two hundred years ago than the modern, tame, stiff apparel, are placed a couple of exceedingly worn out horse-hair sofas, a looking glass with a tarnished gilt frame swathed in yellow gauze; and several chairs, evidently of the same date and origin as the sofas, are ranged in various corners.

"Poor little lad!" says Mr. Ferrier, laying the boy down with gentle hands on one of the sofas. "Hallo! Adolphe, Alphonse, Jean," he calls without in the passage, pausing a moment to apostrophize the porter to have a care of his luggage; "these are common French Christian names, are they not? How deaf these people are! Well, Providence, they say, helps those who help themselves. Can *you* give me some assistance, Mademoiselle?"

Emptying some water from a caraffe standing on the table into a tumbler, he asks Thyrza to hold the glass for him. But when she approaches the sofa she turns sick and faint; the child's face is covered with blood, that has trickled down from the wound in his forehead staining the smart orange scarf, while his eyes are widely distended, without any expression or emotion in the staring balls.

"Je ne puis pas, Monsieur," she stammers, with an involuntary retrograde movement, and nearly letting the tumbler slip from her trembling grasp.

"Just like a woman!" exclaims Mr. Ferrier, in very Anglicized French. "Are you going to faint too, and make a scene? Stand back, Mademoiselle, and let the patient have as much air as can be obtained in this stuffy little room."

A laugh greets this speech, which is more intelligible from the manner of delivery than from the correctness of the grammar, and looking round, Thyrza discovers that the room is by no means so destitute of tenants as it was at first, but on the contrary, is pretty well filled with commis-voyageurs, strolling artists, and one or two actors who belong to a provincial company. They have entered by another door from the salle-à-manger.　Most of them are sallow bearded Frenchmen, and they are gesticulating and vociferating noisily, after the fashion of their country when anything uncommon occurs.

"Take a chair and sit down in comfort—do not stand there looking ready to drop.　I thought at least I was sure of some help in trouble from a woman, even though she may be good for nothing else."

"I am *not* going to faint, Monsieur," she answers, indignantly, in a sweet low voice, which draws the attention of the odd dozen Frenchmen upon her.　Perceiving their eyes fixed in her direction, she flushes scarlet, and wishes profoundly that Mr. Spindler would make haste and deliver her from her embarrassing position among a number of men whom she had never seen before.

"If you are not going to faint, take the handkerchief and sponge like this," showing her how to manipulate the linen, "while I see if that bell over there will ring.　He ought to have a medical man at once."

Thyrza tries to obey, but her nerve fails her on touching the death-like face over which a crimson streak is flowing, and she grasps hold of the back of the chair for support.　She is very angry with her own stupidity—still she cannot help it. If she had been cast in an heroic mould, she would have been mistress of the position in a moment—have bound up the wound without the slightest previous knowledge being necessary, and by her elegance and ease of manner have charmed all the men, including Mr. Ferrier, at once. That is what she ought to have done. Instead of this, she feels supremely *gauche*, awkward, and out of place. With the instinct common to every woman who wishes to appear to the greatest advantage and is painfully conscious of being untidy, she puts her hand up to her head, and looks at herself in the mirror. The result is not flattering to her vanity. By its kindly aid she sees that her hair hangs about her shoulders and waist in rough masses, her collar is crumpled and awry. The fact, also, that she has neither hat nor jacket is palpable, and her brown, ink-stained fingers would be much improved by the addition of a pair of gloves. Mr. Ferrier observes her glance at herself in the mirror. If the reflection in the glass be correct, her complexion is of a greenish-yellow hue, suggestive of recent recovery from jaundice, while one side of her face is swollen considerably larger than the other.

"Not a pretty girl," thinks Mr. Ferrier,

nearly laughing outright at the mortified expression of Thyrza's countenance, " and certainly" (taking into consideration her common dress, made without any attempt at trimming and very little at a fit, being the joint result of the united labours of Miss Holt and herself) " one of the untidiest I ever saw."

But the old yellow gown, baggy and ill-made though it be, cannot wholly conceal the graceful proportions of a slender waist and a figure just rounding into womanhood, while the white collar closes over the soft curves of a smooth brown throat on which the small head is exquisitely set, and the short dress shows dainty little ankles.

" Was there ever anything so utterly foolish, so vain, so frivolous, so *useless* in every sense of the word as a young, silly girl ?" he asks.

" I am not useless, Monsieur," protests Thyrza, with an indignant flash of her hazel eyes.

" The proof of the pudding is in the eating. Pray what can you do ?"

" I can make omelettes, and darn stockings, and teach English, and "—emphatically but vaguely—" oh, heaps of things !"

" Oh, indeed ! But I do not want you to exercise your skill in these matters at present," he answers, bluntly; " what did you come here for?"

" Mr. Spindler sent me to help about the little boy," answers she, twisting her slim, ink-stained fingers together, and forgetting Mr. Ferrier knows nothing of Mr. Spindler.

" An immense deal you have helped, have you not? Well, since you can do nothing else, try and ring the bell."

" I—I shan't," she returns. " Will you?" she asks of one of the Frenchmen who is standing near her. There is a general rush to the bell in compliance with her wishes, and the man who is successful in reaching it first pulls so vigorously that the bell does not stop ringing for more than five minutes when set in motion, and the rope—rotten, no doubt, from age—snaps in two.

The landlady, thus imperatively summoned, quits her cooking operations in the kitchen, and arrives in the billiard-room very red in the face, and bringing with her an overpowering odour of garlic; the landlord, the ostler, and several females present themselves in the doorway, uttering shrill or bass exclamations, according to their sex, of " Mon Dieu!" " Oh, ciel!" " Dame!" and " Sacré!" with a liberal allowance of re's to the latter.

"Where is de leetle knabe?   I hope I haf not killed him!" anxiously inquires Mr. Spindler, waddling into the room.

" Oh, he will come round—have no fear of that," replies Mr. Ferrier, translating literally the English into French. " I have sent one of these duffers for a doctor, and we shall have him right in a trice."

" I no comprehend," says Mr. Spindler. On which Thyrza renders the above into French. *Duffer* is, however, untranslatable. Thyrza, not being versed in English slang, pauses at the word.

" Say bête, or stupid," rejoins Mr. Ferrier; " either word will do."

Mr. Spindler takes a mighty pinch of snuff, and a ray of hope illumines his doleful visage.

" You no think anything will happen to me, sare?" he asks, in his broken English, having detected the British element in the good Samaritan; " I nevare toch him.   I only say 'Andate al diavolo!' and he run and fall on de oder side of the street."

" Your mind may be quite easy on that subject," answers Mr. Ferrier, " especially in a country where the jury always bring in ' extenuating circumstances.' They are a tender-hearted set of people here. They vivisect poor innocent animals in the name and interests of science, and let a fellow off with next to nothing who has perhaps chopped his father and mother into little bits!"

With the kindly presence of Mr. Spindler Thyrza's courage revives. She ventures to unfasten the boy's cravat, and moisten his dry lips with water. Mr. Ferrier asks for some brandy, and pours a small quantity down the child's throat. He has bound up the ghastly wound, but the blood still continues to ooze through the tight bandages.

"That is better," says Mr. Ferrier to Thyrza. "I wish I had had a needle and thread to draw it together with. It would soon heal, and scarcely leave a scar."

At this point the doctor is ushered into the billiard-room. He proceeds to examine the amount of injury the child has sustained, pronounces the bandages to be cleverly arranged, and decides the wound must be stitched up. Then he produces a case of glittering steel instruments, the sight of which causes Thyrza to shiver and shut her eyes, and in a few moments the operation is over. Shortly afterwards, the boy gives a deep sigh, and tries to sit up. He fumbles about with his fingers as if groping for something, and is evidently searching for the guinea-pig. Thyrza lifts it out of his pocket, and places it in his hands. A smile of intelligence lights up the thin countenance. He feels his pet, and strokes it carefully. It is not hurt in any way.

"Lie still, little man. You will be able to get up to-morrow, but you must rest for the present. Will you tell him, Mademoiselle? He cannot make out my French."

"He is alive—he no die!" exclaims Mr. Spindler, joyfully. "I dance for happiness!"

So saying, on the spur of the moment he executes several pirouettes of delight at the relief to his feelings, which Mr. Ferrier regards much as Michal regarded the triumphal dancing of David before the ark.

"I pay this gentleman for his attendance on the knabe," continues Mr. Spindler, pulling out his purse, and addressing himself to the doctor.

"Not at all—allow me," interrupted Mr. Ferrier; "it was purely an accident. You had nothing to do with it."

"I will look in to-morrow and inquire how he is," persists Mr. Spindler.

"By all means, and I daresay you can contrive to get him apprenticed to some decent employment to save him from going about the country begging his bread. There is nothing further for you to do," adds Mr. Ferrier, coolly ; " so, I wish you bon jour. Thank you, Mademoiselle, for your valuable services," with a mischievous look in his steel-grey eyes. " Shall you return by the window in the same way as you came ?"

Thyrza would willingly part with her most precious possession in exchange for a witty and crushing reply wherewith to extinguish Ferrier, but having no answer ready, she merely answers, " Adieu, Monsieur."

As she and Mr. Spindler go back to the *pension*, the lady of the green gown passes by them into the hotel, and asks if the landlady can supply her with apartments.

CHAPTER II.

THERE has just been a shower of rain; the clouds have cleared away; the sun shines brightly again; the air is sweet and balmy; grey and golden-brown-dressed sparrows chirp gaily as they fly under the eaves of the *pension*, with long ends of straw dangling from their bills; the blackbirds sing in the apple boughs, while they think of the surreptitious feasts they will have in the summer on the juicy cherries and ripe strawberries; and the " silver spears " of rain-drops still fall pattering through the thick leaves. From where Thyrza is sitting, perched on a twisted branch of an old apple-tree that bears nothing in the autumn save a few sour dwarf green apples, she can see little beyond a sea of soft rose-tinted blossoms. Right across, divided by the river, half a dozen paces from her, stretch acres upon acres of pink-and-white orchards, only varied by the fresh green foliage that is rejoicing in its escape from its winter shroud. To the left lies the town of Villios, grey and hoary, with red-tiled roofs to most of the houses, some of which having lately been repaired, turn into bright scarlet in the rays of the evening sun. Some distance nearer is the narrow Norman bridge, beneath which the river flows tranquilly to the sea, bearing on its breast the faded petals of " angel" blue forget-me-nots, and the swans, like those on " still St. Mary's lake, float double—swan and shadow." Close beside the bridge is a blacksmith's forge: the clink, clink of the hammer comes musically across the river, red sparks fly out at the door; blanchisseuses are wringing linen in the water; two or three boys are fishing with willow wands as rods, their breeches tucked up above their knees; behind is the terraced gardens of the *pension*, its stiff, straight, formal walks, its cloisters and gables.

Miss Holt, the head of the *pension*, is at tea with her pupils. Thyrza is generally hungry, as it is given only to schoolgirls and schoolboys to be; but on this evening her appetite has deserted her, and she is enjoying the sweets of her favourite seat—a forbidden pleasure, and in consequence a much prized and doubly precious one.

In a short time she will be obliged to go into the house to superintend the younger pupils preparing their lessons, while she mends the house linen. Having reached the mature age of seventeen her education is supposed to be finished, and as Miss Holt gives out she receives but little money in payment for her board, Thyrza in return saves Miss Holt the expense of employing a junior English teacher; and Mr. Spindler, out of disinterested friendship, continues gratuitously his music lessons.

In July the holidays begin, but there will not be much amusement for Thyrza: she will be left alone in the *pension* with old Mère Pantouffle, while Miss Holt is enjoying herself in London or Brighton. Being an orphan without a fortune, Thyrza has her own way to make. Occasionally she has visions of going to Stuttgardt, as Mr. Spindler suggests, to study music and become a professional. Anything will be better than droning out her existence in this dead-alive *pension*: it would even be pleasanter to be a housemaid or one of the peasant women who work hard in the fields, for they are independent and can earn money, whilst Thyrza never knows what it is to call a sixpence her own, and for years has never had a new dress, always wearing Miss Holt's old ones. Ah! if she could only go to Stuttgardt! But then, where is the money to come from? To be sure, she does not want for relations. She has several uncles and aunts, all married and well-to-do in the world, and provided with more or less numerous families; but Mr. and Mrs. Rutherfurd having offended their people by their marriage, Thyrza shrinks from asking for their assistance.

Mr. and Mrs. Rutherfurd had made an imprudent match and married on about ninety pounds a year. Mr. Rutherfurd was a gentleman born, the younger son of the Rutherfurds of High Riggs, a well-known Scotch family of distinction. Dreamy, enthusiastic, always building improbable speculations as to what he would do if he had " time to look about him," impractical, unpunctual, a mere child in business matters, John Rutherfurd was totally unfitted to fight his way through a contest in which the weakest go to the wall. Both he and his wife having seriously displeased their relatives by their marriage, when impecunious times came both husband and wife vainly appealed to their people for assistance. Mrs. Rutherfurd's sister had married a captain in the navy, called Salton, now appointed Inspecting Commander of Her Majesty's Coastguard at Marshley-on-the-Wolds in L——shire.   Captain and Mrs. Salton were well off, but their opinion was that Mrs. Rutherfurd had chosen her lot, and now she must make the best of it.   She had been deaf to good advice, and must reap the consequences.   Mr. and Mrs. Rutherfurd found the consequences by no means pleasant.   Love may have sufficed for all wants in a past age, but it certainly does not in this age of prosaic realities.   At last, through the interest of a friend in Shanghai, a situation as clerk in a bank in that city was offered to Mr. Rutherfurd, which he was glad enough to accept; and accordingly, eighteen years before this little sketch begins, Mr. and Mrs. Rutherfurd went out to China.   After a brief sojourn in Shanghai Mrs. Rutherfurd succumbed to the fever of the country, and a few months later Mr. Rutherfurd followed her to the grave, leaving little Thyrza a legacy to whomsoever would take charge of her.

One of Mr. Rutherfurd's friends, a young merchant, Luke Mark by name, goodnaturedly undertook the care of the child, and bringing her over to Europe, placed her on the recommendation of a clergyman, whose daughters Miss Holt had educated, at the *pension* of S. Sebastian the Martyr.   But who provides the money defraying the expenses of her education, Thyrza does not know. A small sum has hitherto been paid regularly, and Miss Holt never fails to remind the girl that she especially ought to behave herself, and feel deeply grateful, for she has been taught and fed on next door to charity.

Mr. Mark, occupied with his business and mercantile transactions in China, never wrote to her; and Thyrza, on her part, did not trouble him with letters. The years and the seasons came and went: spring wore into summer; June roses bloomed and faded; autumn's harvests were garnered, and winter's cold winds returned, but no letters, and no relations ever visited the dull *pension* in the quaint town of Villios, where Thyrza spent her childish days. Other girls grew up and left school; they had their friends, their fathers and mothers, and sisters and brothers. Thyrza's wistful dark eyes often filled with tears, and her face had a strange hungry look when she saw the happy family parties that assembled at the Christmas and Midsummer holidays. The girls frequently invited her to pay them visits at their homes, but Miss Holt invariably objected. How could Thyrza go gadding about out visiting when she had no clothes and no money to spare? It was a likely thing that she (Miss Holt) could afford to give Thyrza railway tickets! Did she not, as it was, keep her merely out of

kindness because she was a waif and stray, of
no consequence to any one; a creature who, if
she died to-morrow, would never be missed
from the world's stage? Thyrza might be very
thankful to have so good a home as the *pension*.
What had she to complain of? Well, when
put down and classified on paper, perhaps not
much, but to a warm-hearted girl like Thyrza,
life with Miss Holt is simply starvation. She
is just at the age when sympathy and kindness
are everything, and Miss Holt has about as much
sympathy for the little whims and vanities of
Thyrza as a piece of stone has for the lichen
which covers it. " If I could but make money !"
she muses, as she sits in the apple-tree and
watches a fat bumble-bee drowsily buzzing from
a pink-scented chaliced flower to a carmine
opening bud; and the shadows of the bridge are
reflected—massive piers and grotesque carvings—
on the smooth, shining surface of the sleepy river,
without a single quiver or ripple to mar the
perfection of the duplicate. Below, a sharp-
nosed water-rat sidles cautiously along among
the tall-bladed grasses; the scentless dog-violets
and golden-marsh marigolds splash into the
water; then the bubbles burst; the circles
diverge, each one growing wider than the last,
until they are stranded and wrecked upon an

islet of water-lily leaves. The sun is westering towards the vineyard-covered mountains; the spring twilight slowly creeps up, and the flush of rosy brilliance fades out from the grey gables of the old *pension*, the many storied houses, and the warm rich red tones of the peaked, sloping roofs. The boys have left off fishing; the eldest of them forms them into a regiment of soldiers, placing himself at their head; they shoulder the willow wands as rifles:

> "Aux armes : citoyens!
>   Formez vos bataillons.
>   Marchez! marchez! qu'un sang impur
>   Abreuve nos sillons."

A strong-minded British female tourist, intent upon "doing" Villios, and getting the full value of her money, looks up from the immortal "Murray" in which she reads—"Villios built time of the Goths, &c.," to remonstrate with the blanchisseuses who are beating the linen violently with good sized stones. They pay no attention to her interference; she resolves not to patronize the Villios washerwomen.

How do other people make money, wonders Thyrza; and what can she do towards obtaining her purpose. She is not clever and can do nothing particularly well. She is not even certain that she has a real talent for music.

Then she is by no means pretty, and has not pleasing manners, nor yet the taste and sense when to say and do the right thing. One may say the right thing, but it is useless to do so ten minutes too late. The difficulty is to judge when *is* the exact moment. Thyrza sighs and comes to the conclusion she will "just have" to go on in the old groove for the remainder of her days, unless something very extraordinary happens such as occurred this morning.

How rude the strange gentleman was! He was not at all like a hero. To have made the adventure complete, he ought to have been nearly seven feet high, handsome as Apollo, gallant as Launcelot, chivalrous as King Arthur; au contraire, he is of the ordinary height, has grey hair, and even in the palmy days of his youth could never by any possibility whatsoever have been called a fine looking man. · As to Thyrza, what a chance she has lost of distinguishing herself. "Time is, time was." The golden opportunity has slipped from her. All she has done creditably was jumping out of the window. That did not take her an instant to accomplish. Suppose some kind uncle should conveniently depart this life, and leave to his dear niece and kinswoman, Thyrza Rutherfurd, his fortune and worldly goods! Delicious idea! what costumes and ravishing toilettes would Thyrza invest in! what gloves and boots! No more of Miss Holt's discarded dresses which never fitted her, and made her look as though she had stuffed the body of her gown with the table-cloth! No more teaching, and mending, and hard words, and sour looks. She will give presents to Mr. Spindler and M. Paul, the barber, who, on a certain memorable occasion unknown to Miss Holt, took Thyrza to the theatre; she will have a carriage and a pair of ponies, and go on a travelling expedition round the world. Most girls marry, she reflected; no one will marry her. She is not beautiful enough, so the fortune will compensate her for a lover—reasoning which wiser persons than Thyrza have arrived at, if the numerous applications for *solatium* in breach of promise cases may be taken as a criterion. And she will have—well, everyone builds castles in the air, not more substantial, and often about as probable of realization as Thyrza's château en Espagne. But how sweet and pleasant are these dreams! No annoyances; no petty vexations; no worrying trifles enter into their airy halls. We do not calculate for them. Lying under a wide-spreading beech tree, blowing a cloud on a summer day:—in that cozy armchair over the fire after some '48 Port;—coming home after that splendid spin with the hounds; rocking lazily as a sunlit sea at the bottom of the boat, with that companion of our joys and troubles, the sharer in our triumphs and down-falls—our pipe, we build charming fabrics of what we will do when we get that money, that living, that "step," that appointment. After all, if it came true, would the reality be half as fair as our pictured vision? Does anything ever come up to our expectations? When the desire of our soul is granted unto us, we often find it valueless. What we thought a precious stone lying among the green fern fronds and veronicas is only a piece of common glass, not worth the exertion of stooping to pick up; the gold we fancied we had found is dross; what we bartered our honour and truth away for, rewards us with perfidy; the fruit that tempts us with its soft luscious ex-terior is full of bitterness. The most brilliant and perfect creations of brush or pen fall far short of that still more beautiful original in the artist's brain, which not embodied in the concrete is probably invested in proportion with superior charms.

There is the half-hour striking from the church tower, whose pinnacles "prick" the evening sky. Thyrza ought to have been in the school-room long ago. She looks out of the apple branches, and, to her horror, sees Miss Holt walking straight down to her pet tree. Adieu vache veau! We know how poor Alnaschar mourned over the destruction of his future hopes, in the City of Roses. Thyrza hastily gathers up the skirt of the canary-coloured dress, spotted thickly with large black dots the size of a half-crown piece, and prepares for war. With ordinary good fortune, Miss Holt ought not to discover Thyrza's vicinity; but, as ill-luck will have it, part of the canary skirt flutters into view. The Byron Thyrza has abstracted from Miss Holt's shelves falls precipitately on to the ground, and a peal of girlish laughter is heard apparently from the depths of the tree. What will Miss Holt say to the Byron? Thyrza has been told on no consideration to read it, and of course has experienced the greatest wish, like Eve, to see what it is like, and why it is wicked. Further concealment is useless.

"Thyrza! I am astonished at your behaviour! You are too old now for these tomboy tricks."

A beaming brown face appears from among clusters of shell-tinted white, perfumed apple-blossoms, fresh and bright as the flowers themselves, and bubbling over with irrepressible merriment.

"Do you want me, Miss Holt?" she inquires, meekly, aware she is overdue for her duties in the school-room by three-quarters of an hour.

"Oh, Thyrza!" shaking her head slowly and mournfully, "you will come to no good if you go on in this way! A young woman at your time of life, who has no fortune to look to, ought to prepare herself for all emergencies. What will become of you?"

"Don't know, and don't care."

"Don't care was hanged," says Miss Holt.

"Then they can't hang him again," returns Thyrza. "If the worst comes to the worst, why, I will sweep a crossing, or perhaps come out as a coryphée," hoping this will shock Miss Holt, in which aspiration her wishes succeed. Miss Holt *is* horrified. She turns up the whites of her eyes towards the setting sun in a pious manner, and sighs profoundly. Evidently much consoled by this exhibition of her religious feelings, she renews the point with Thyrza, who is forced to spring down from her refuge. She descends with merely the accident of tearing some folds of the dreadful canary garment from the gathers. At this mishap she involuntarily gives a prolonged whistle; she is fully cognizant of the fact this is a shockingly unladylike, improper, and most reprehensible habit—an accomplishment not heard of in Miss Holt's young days—and, in general, it has the effect upon that lady which shaking a red rag has upon a bull. She looks grave; Thyrza's sins and offences are great. She is too old now to be shut up in a dark room all day, with the invigorating diet of bread and water as a consolation, in which manner some dreary hours of her childhood have been passed. With commendable presence of mind Thyrza picks up the Byron, very nearly indulging in a farewell whistle, but checking herself in time, she stands still to hear what Miss Holt has got to say.

Miss Holt has watched the descent of her junior English teacher from the tree with suppressed impatience. Spare, neat, angular, lynx-eyed, she is the terror of the *pension* domestics, of the Villios tradespeople, and of the gardener especially, who at this moment is leaning on his spade, not even *attempting* to work, as she would have remarked if she had spoken her thoughts aloud. If Miss Holt could have had her own way, and arranged the world according to *her* ideas, the flowers should have toiled and spun for their bright robes, and the birds have done something for their living besides making the earth glad with their songs. Being so industrious herself, the *dolce far niente* is to her an unutterable abomination; people who are delicate, or possessed of nerves, she does not believe in, setting them down as humbugs. On her looking at the gardener, he thinks it advisable to make a show of working, and towards executing this object inserts his spade into the ground in a languid manner, which causes Miss Holt to long to give him a good shaking on the spot.

"I have got a letter for you, Thyrza."

"A letter for *me!*" exclaims Thyrza, "wonders will never cease," as Miss Holt hands her an epistle, duly addressed to "Miss Thyrza Rutherfurd, care of Miss Holt, Pension de S. Sebastian the Martyr, Département ——, France." Miss Holt has opened it, and made herself acquainted with the contents, which are to this effect:—

LILLIESHILL, *May 17th*, 1872.

"DEAR MISS RUTHERFURD,—As I imagine you must now be verging upon that important period when young ladies leave school, I have been thinking about what is to be done regarding your future. I came home from China viâ San Francisco and New York, that being a more convenient way than the other round by the Suez Canal, or I should have taken a look at Paris and come on to see you, and the good lady who has been so kind to you. Since my arrival at Lillieshill I have written to several of your relations, as they are your natural protectors, but they tell me they have as much as they can do to bring up their own families; of course I can have no idea about your capabilities or what plans you may have formed for yourself; however, I may mention a friend of mine in the neighbourhood of Lillieshill is in want of a governess for her children. She is an extremely amiable woman, and at any rate you would have a good comfortable home. Whether you decide upon accepting the situation or not, I shall be glad to see you; and my uncle and aunt, Mr. and Miss Lefroy, with whom I am staying for the present, hope you will come and spend two or three weeks with us. I am not sure if I have ever told you so before, but I am not your guardian, although I have in a measure virtually acted that part. I knew your poor father well, and should be happy for his sake to see his daughter advantageously settled in life. I have written to Miss Holt, enclosing a cheque for the last six months of your education, &c., and also another for your journey money: should there be more than you require spend it on any trifle you may fancy. I shall be going up to town within a fortnight, and hope therefore that you will start as soon (if possible) as you receive this note. With kind regards, and hoping you will manage your travels in safety. I have given Miss Holt full particulars on the subject, which I have no doubt she will explain to you.

"Believe me, yours truly,

"LUKE MARK.

"P.S.—Address, Lillieshill, near Queensmuir, Kilniddryshire, Scotland. I see I forgot to write the full address at the beginning of my letter, so to prevent mistakes give it now."

"I don't want to go," says Thyrza, with the natural perversity of human nature; now the object of her longings is within her grasp, it suddenly loses its piquant flavour, till at once the *pension* becomes dear to her. Miss Holt seems her best friend; the very pile of linen waiting in the school-room for her unwilling fingers to darn the wide and frequent rents and thin places is invested with a fresh light. They are all old familiar acquaintances; through force of habit she has become accustomed to them, and they to her—one cannot say attached, for it would be difficult for Miss Holt to inspire any one with affection; she is hard and dry, and never called human being *darling* in the fifty odd years that have elapsed since Maria Holt

first saw the light. A long series of disappoint-
ments will wear creases in the softest and
sweetest disposition.

"Don't be ridiculous, Thyrza," answers Miss
Holt, testily. "You will have to go. Mr.
Mark has paid for your school expenses himself.
Now he is tired of doing so, and consequently
wishes you to work for yourself."

"I wonder if he would let me go to Stuttgardt,"
says Thyrza, in a meditative voice.

"Nonsense! Who is to support you while
you are studying? Come into the house at
once, and I will get you a box, and help you
to pack. It is a pity I must lose you. I shall
not be so well suited again."

Miss Holt is quite right. It will be some
time before she obtains such a convenient
pupil as Thyrza; one whose money she can
pocket, and no awkward questions be asked.
They enter the school-room, where a busy
murmur of voices is heard from the girls learning
their lessons for the following day. In the
next room a small child is practising the minor
scale of A. She plays the notes irregularly.
They come in scrambling like a flock of sheep.
In another apartment some one is studying
Gounod's march from Faust, and a third a
lively Scotch air; all three sounds, the doleful

scale of A minor; the soldier's chorus; the light tunes, jar and jangle with each other. There is the chair Thyrza ought to have occupied, and the big clothes' basket with its freight ready to be repaired. Mademoiselle Lambert, an elderly person with a long nose, black eyes, very thin hair much covered with pomade, and an erection of red silk on the top of her head, has supplied her place. She is devouring a novel called " Georgine," and says warningly, " S-sh ! Marie, vous ne faites rien" as Miss Holt and Thyrza pass through the school-room.

" Would not you like to return to me, Thyrza, after your visit to Scotland ?" asks Miss Holt, who has been pondering deeply how inconvenient it is to part with Thyrza, and wondering when she will be able again to pick up so cheap a bargain.

" No, thank you, Miss Holt," answers Thyrza, firmly. Her momentary regret has passed away into a sensation of joy and delight at the prospect of release from the prison-house of the *pension*, and glowing expectations of what will happen out in the world, of which she knows so little, and paints to herself in such brilliant colours.

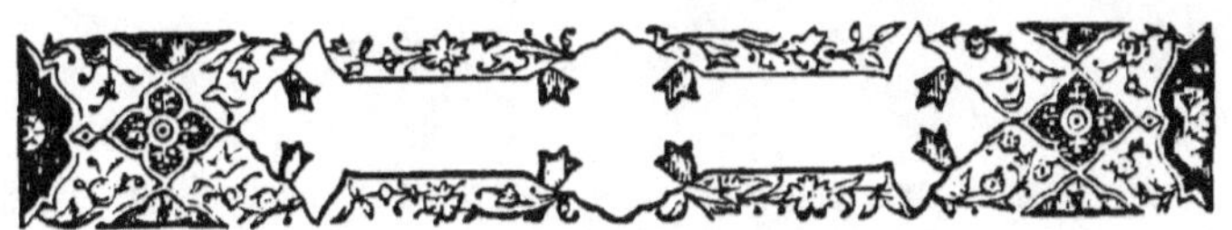

CHAPTER III.

GOING away, Thyrza ?   What will become of me without my best pupil ?" laments Mr. Spindler.

He is standing at the door of the Flying Dragon, whither the diligence in which Thyrza is seated has returned from the *pension* in order to pick up Madame Dawson's luggage. Madame Dawson is the lady with the green satin dress and ruby velvet bonnet whom Thyrza watched arrive the morning before, from Trois d'Or. She came for the purpose of installing two of her children under Miss Holt's fostering care, and to-day she is going to travel as far as Paris. To-morrow she goes to Calais, and will cross from thence to Dover. She intends making some stay in London. Miss Holt has asked that Thyrza may accompany her to London, where she is to spend a night, starting for Scotland from King's Cross by the 10 A.M. train the following morning. As yet Thyrza has not been introduced to Madame Dawson; but the pleasure is not to be much longer postponed, for she sees the green folds of a satin dress, rustling down the passage where yesterday she followed Mr. Ferrier into the billiard-room.

"Oh, you will soon get another pupil," says Thyrza.

"Not one like you; so good, so attentive," he sighed.

"And who is so fond of her darling old master," smiles Thyrza. "I am *so* sorry to leave you, Mr. Spindler. You have always been very kind to me."

"Thou wilt write, Thyrza, and tell me how thou gettest on when far away from Villios? Once I go to Edinburgh to see a friend whom I first knew in Stuttgardt. We studied together at the Conservatorium, and he was Kapel-Meister for two years to the king. But jealousy came, and his enemies made poor Louis leave Stuttgardt and go to Scotland. On week days it was all very well in Edinburgh, but on the Sundays it was too awful! After I had been to my chapel, I had nothing to do. If you play the piano on the Sunday you will have a whole crowd round the house. Ach! I *live* de oder days, but on the Sundays I only *wegetate!*"

"We may as well say good-bye now," says Miss Holt; "it will soon be time for you to give Mademoiselle Thibault her lesson."

"Lebewohl, Thyrza," says Mr. Spindler, lapsing, according to his wont when carried away by his feelings, into his beloved harmonious German, "take care of thyself and forget not the old man" (shaking hands heartily). "When I publish my étude on Scotch airs, it shall be dedicated to thee, Rösleinroth."

"Good-bye, Mr. Spindler. I will practise the sonatas regularly, and will only get some of Ascher's music as a treat to refresh me," answers Thyrza, warmly. Mr. Spindler does not much approve of Ascher; brilliant and dashing without solidity or thoroughness, is his opinion of that composer's writings.

He moves a step forward and shakes his head in deprecation of Thyrza's pretended preference (she has only said so to teaze him) of Ascher's music over the sublime works of Mozart, Haydn, Beethoven, and Handel.

"Lebewohl, Thyrza!" he repeats, tenderly and reluctantly. Dear old Mr. Spindler, who has initiated Thyrza into the mysteries and art of music, from reading her notes and the five-finger exercise to the "Moonlight Sonata" and Bach's Passion music, she would give him a kiss were not Miss Holt and Mr. Ferrier standing on the doorsteps looking at her. She does not mind Miss Holt in the least; to her she has shaken off all allegiance and obedience, and is free as air or the wave on the sea, and can no longer be called to account for bad behaviour. But when she reaches down to where short, fat Mr. Spindler stands, sadness depicted on his face, a large snuff-box in his hand, a ray of sunshine sloping through the tiny slit of blue heaven visible between the red roofs of the high storied houses touching his venerable head with silver, she catches a look of extreme amusement in Mr. Ferrier's grey eyes. She draws hastily back into the diligence; Mr. Ferrier is smoking a cigar, a cloud of smoke goes curling up into the air by the vermilion and gold sign of the Flying Dragon. At his side is the little Italian, his head bound up across his brow, but otherwise looking the picture of mirth and health. The guinea-pig is adorned with a collar and small chain now; a safer arrangement than that of allowing it to be at liberty.

Mr. Spindler would fain say more, but as he begins to speak, Madame Dawson, closely veiled, sails out under the porch, and Miss Holt approaching to effect the introduction, he is almost demolished and swept away by the tide

of wide, flowing petticoats and insubordinate
crinolines.

Miss Holt kisses Thyrza for the first and the
last time since she has dwelt within the walls of
S. Sebastian the Martyr. After all, she will
miss the girl with her picturesque face, her
gentle manners, and untidy ways; the *pension*
will not seem itself for a few days without
Thyrza, who has been so long a tenant of its
dark, sombre rooms. Perhaps, too, the recollection of sundry meannesses practised on the
unsuspecting child occurs to her mind reproachfully. It is very inconvenient too for the junior
English teacher to take her departure so much
before the holidays begin. However, one cannot
always regulate these little *contretemps* to one's
liking, and, on the whole, Miss Holt has made
an extremely good thing out of Thyrza.

Madame Dawson is successfully launched into
the diligence, and expresses her happiness at
making Thyrza's acquaintance.

Mr. Spindler once more attempts to speak,
but Miss Holt promptly interferes, and he retires, muttering to himself in German under his
breath. The door is closed now and the rickety
vehicle is about to start, when Mr. Ferrier flings
away the remains of his cigar, and running up to
the diligence, places one foot on the step that

assists you to climb up, and gives Thyrza a beautiful Gloire de Dijon rose. It is only the middle of May, so it must have been forced in a hothouse. Madame Dawson clearly thinks it is intended for her, and wishes to take it from Thyrza, but Mr. Ferrier says distinctly, " C'est pour Mademoiselle Thyrza," continuing more fluently in English, " I regret it is such a poor flower. Keep it in remembrance——shall I say of a *disagreeable* man ?"

" Thanks, Monsieur," returns Thyrza, lighting up with a smile that displays two rows of pearly white teeth.

The driver cracks his whip, the wretched horses move, and in another moment Thyrza is driving at a jog-trot through Villios. A few minutes more and she will leave the old-fashioned town and all its historic associations behind. It is an ancient town, which carries one back to the splendour and chivalry of a past century, when brilliant cavalcades rode through the narrow streets; when courtiers placed all their fortunes in ropes of pearls and jewels on their clothes; when the king was secure on his throne, feasting in marble palaces, and the peasants died by scores in misery, after lives of abject toil and poverty. A town with a thousand memories, and a great solemn cathedral still

consecrated by the fervent prayers breathed out
on its chequered stone pavements by pious souls
in times gone past; a grey town, with dried up
moats round its massive ramparts filled with
cherry trees—at present one cloud of scented
snow; a peaceful town, with a broad, sleepy,
apple-orchard bordered river, beyond which comes
a rich, fertile, corn-growing country; a land
indeed flowing with milk and honey, and girt
in and bounded by a low range of vineyard-
clothed hills.

Mr. Ferrier has gone into the billiard-room in
the hotel; but Mr. Spindler and M. Paul, the
Villios barber and coiffeur *par excellence*, watch
the diligence until a turn of the street hides
both them and the Flying Dragon, from sight.
As the diligence whisks round the sharp corner,
Thyrza waves her handkerchief; whether Mr.
Spindler sees it or not she cannot tell.

It is market day. The travellers pass many
carts containing butter, and cheese, and milk,
and spring vegetables of various kinds. Jogging
along the dusty roads with their patient beasts of
burden, are several peasants who sometimes stop
at a rain-begrimed weather-beaten stone fountain,
surmounted by a figure of the Madonna and Child,
to refresh their thirsty animals. Villios and its pink
and white apple orchards, its large river, good Mr.

Spindler and the *pension* where Thyrza has passed twelve years of her existence, dwindle and lessen in the distance.

Madame Dawson complains of a *migraine,* declares the odour of a huge bouquet of flowers, a gift to Thyrza from some of her school friends, is *étouffante.*   She has the windows first opened and then shut; she deluges herself with eau-de-Cologne and Jockey Club, and is altogether restless and uncomfortable.   At Trois d'Or several passengers alight, leaving only a commis-voyageur and two soldiers in the conveyance with Madame and Thyrza.   The soldiers discuss the late war and abuse *ces cochons des Prussiens.*   The commis-voyageur explains his belief that if *he* had been at the head of affairs things would have been very different.   Why did not Bazaine make a sortie from Metz?   But the generals conspired among themselves to sell France to the enemy, and they ought all to have been shot for their treachery.   Marshal Macmahon was the only patriot among them.   As for the Man of Sedan, nothing could excuse his conduct or exonerate him from the charge of the blackest ingratitude to France, who had made his fortune and raised him from obscurity.   The soldiers do not agree.   They blame the generals also; but they are unanimous in asserting, that the Emperor was deceived by his ministers regarding the state of the army.

While changing horses at Trois d'Or, they go into the hotel to partake of coffee with a dash of brandy in it. There is no railway either to Villios or Trois d'Or, so the diligence proceeds to Rougeville, from whence there is a direct line to Paris. The soldiers and commis-voyageur return to resume their argument; under cover of the sound of their voices, Madame waxes confidential, and tells Thyrza her history. As far as can be seen through the black veil, she is a very handsome woman with bright yellow hair, pretty nearly the colour of Thyrza's obnoxious and detested canary gown now safely stowed away at the very bottom of her box. By birth she is an Andalusian. Her husband was a poor English artist, who had nothing but his pencil on which to depend for bread and cheese. He came to a small village in Andalusia on a holiday expedition, seeking subjects for an academy picture. Madame was the belle of the village. She sat to Mr. Dawson in various characters as model. Mr. Dawson fell in love. Being under the impression she would be taken to rich England and live on the fat of the land, Madame thought she would try the experiment. It was preferable to marrying poor Carlos, the muleteer. But what

eyes Carlos had! and what a devoted heart!
So Madame and Mr. Dawson went to the little
church of San Juan, on the hillside near the
village, and were married. And Carlos became
a brigand, and was shot while pillaging an
English milord. A bad ending!—not at all.
Far more poetical than if he had borne his
reverse with fortitude, and eventually married
Violante, the wealthy olive merchant's daughter,
who would have given her fingers for him.
However, Madame had reckoned her chickens
before they were hatched, and Mr. Augustus
Dawson and she lived in cheap lodgings in a
part of Paris generally known as the Quartier
Latin, the favourite residence of artists, stu-
dents, and literary people of a Bohemian taste.
Madame evidently disliked that portion of her
life. It was not what she had expected, and
was slower than the Andalusian village where
she danced boleros with Carlos, and broke the
hearts of half the young fellows in the neighbourhood. She thought that with her personal
advantages she ought to have made a better
match than "pauvre Auguste," who had blindly
adored her.

"I wanted to go to the theatre and amuse
myself when he was busy working—it was always
work, work with him—but he would never let

me," mourns Madame. During the past year he overworked himself over a large picture intended for the English Academy, and before it was hung his health gave way completely, and he died. The very day of his death news came from England that an old aunt, who during her lifetime had steadily refused him assistance, had gone to that bourne whence no traveller—in spite of what Home and the spiritualists may urge to the contrary—has been known, at least in modern times, to return, leaving him nearly a hundred thousand pounds. The good fortune came too late. A little of that wealth a few months earlier might have saved him; but the man was dying, the sands of life were fast running out. He was just able to scrawl a few words and sign his name, willing all his property away to his "beloved Preciosa," when he died.

"And he is buried in Père la Chaise," continues Madame, cheerfully, " in what Auguste used to call a ' *nice snog* ' spot."

" Shall you go and see his grave when we pass through Paris?" asks Thyrza, with respect for Madame's sorrow.

" Ah! no," says Madame, fanning herself languidly and glancing with complacence on the superb diamond and ruby bracelets she had bought with " pauvre Auguste's" money. " Ah!

no. It makes me so *triste*. It can do Auguste
no good. I do not like the tristesse ! It gives
me a *migraine*. And many *migraines* spoil the
complexion !"

After this Madame Dawson goes off comfortably to sleep, nodding up and down as the
unwieldy lumbering diligence slips from one rut
into another. While Thyrza, left to her own
reflections, gazes dreamily at the fields of young
growing wheat and maize; the chapels and
hamlets; the wayside crosses and images of the
Madonna ; here and there a small plantation of
trees ; the pointed extinguisher towers of a
nobleman's château, which seem to flit by in
the eight miles that divide Trois d'Or from
Rougeville. The presence of a large and flourishing manufacturing town is denoted by the
increasing number of houses of importance, and
by the dense smoke rising high above the tall
brick chimneys, and resting like a pillar of cloud
over the city.

At the station Madame is awakened from
her slumbers by the halting of the diligence.
Thyrza and she gather together her numerous
maps and divers reticules, scent-bottles, novels,
&c., for beguiling the tedium of the journey, and
almost immediately afterwards they are added to
the number of caged individuals in the waiting-

room, where several distracted and irritated Britons, withheld from the privilege of parading up and down the platform, are becoming furious, threatening complaints to the heads of the police and the managers of the railway company.

Madame's appearance creates quite a sensation, which apparently is rather gratifying to her than otherwise. For she takes it all very quietly, settles herself at once into a more becoming attitude than she troubled herself to assume when left in the diligence with only Thyrza and the soldiers as spectators; arranges the strings of the minute velvet gipsy bonnet under her soft white chin; runs her fingers, covered with jewels, through the meshes of her exceedingly golden locks; shakes the folds of her dress so as to display the point of a bronze kid boot, and swings slowly backwards and forwards a large black Spanish fan.

The men put up their eyeglasses and stare: the women stare too, study the cut of Madame's apparel, which is certainly perfection: the dress which shows through a transparent Chantilly lace shawl, thrown carelessly back, fitting like a second skin to the magnificently developed bust and grandly proportioned neck and shoulders; and then they draw away their petticoats from contact with Madame's skirt.

Madame sees it well enough. She endeavours to remove the thick black Shetland veil she has hitherto worn, which has concealed her features completely, making it an impossibility to know whether the mask hides a face hideous as the veiled prophet's, or one rivalling the Venus de' Medici in beauty.

"Will Mademoiselle Thyrza help me to unfasten this?" she asks, after attempting in vain to untie the knot with her left hand, on the wedding finger of which she wears the correct plain gold ring, and above, a keeper of diamonds.

One of the waiting-room windows looks out upon a sort of country, and at the back of the station. In this, six workmen are having their dinner, on a rude table, constructed out of a plank of wood resting on two unequal sticks, not very securely fixed in the ground. Their meal consists of huge chunks of brown, nearly black bread; raw turnips, carrots, and cheese, washed down by draughts of weak cold tea. They are all of them fine, well grown specimens of men; tall, broad shouldered, lengthy of limb, brawny of muscle; their arms, bared above the elbow, are white as a woman's, and the blue veins and muscles stand out like whipcord. They have come from near the Black Forest to seek

employment, and are natives of the Harz Mountains. Thyrza, sitting near the window, cannot
help observing them; she moves out of sight;
then comes back to see if they are still there;
moves again; returns; meets their eyes; at this
game of Bo-peep they laugh, and Thyrza, smiling also, goes towards Madame Dawson.

Accordingly, after some little difficulty, she
unties the knot: Madame murmurs her thanks;
folding the veil, she places it in her reticule,
and turns on Thyrza the' loveliest countenance
she ever beheld. Features cut like those of a
Greek statue: dazzling white skin with a soft
peach bloom upon it: a mouth like an Apollo's
bow; eyes of the hue of blue cornflowers or
sapphires, whichever simile you may prefer, and
yellow hair of a profusion and brightness which
seems as though it must certainly owe more to
art than nature.

The women are stagnated at Madame's assurance, and retire as far as is possible, without
being markedly uncivil, but Madame does not
care. She has the admiration and attention of
every man in the room concentrated upon her,
and she can afford to despise the unfeigned
dislike and opprobrium of her own sex. Besides,
what is the admiration of a score of women,
compared with the compliments of even one

man? Thyrza envies Madame her *sangfroid* and *nonchalance.* How charmingly she would have played the part of heroine yesterday, in which Thyrza failed so lamentably. Madame would not have been *gauche* and stupid: she would have had some *jeu d'esprit* with which to extinguish Mr. Ferrier, when he made such rude remarks. The door being thrown open, puts an end to the little silent pantomime, and there is an universal rush for seats. One of the Englishmen who has stormed so violently concerning his forced detention in the waiting-room, a big blonde man who, like the gentleman in *Punch* has "grown through his hair," occupies one corner of Madame's coupé. He has a handsome, rather baby-face, with not much expression in his countenance, and enters into conversation with Madame, whose beauty has made a deep impression upon him. He speaks French as well as Madame does English; but presently Madame begins talking in the latter language. No one takes the slightest notice of Thyrza, of which she is not sorry; for it is a sight in itself to witness Madame's gestures: her exact knowledge of the way she shows to most advantage; leaning her head on one hand with the black fan half closed, as a set-off to the delicate contour of her regular profile and Titianlike colouring : then looking round suddenly, with a smile that parts the half-pouting scarlet lips just enough and no more.

What would Mr. Ferrier have thought of her, reflects Thyrza. To be sure, he would have admired her. To a person of his rough blunt exterior, her voluptuous style would be especially captivating. How odd of him to have given her the rose! He did not seem a pleasant man; yet he was very kind and gentle with the small Italian, and no woman's hands could have gone to work more softly or carefully than did his.

Madame chatters and laughs, eats bonbons from a tiny box embroidered with gold and set with turquoises. The Englishman pulls his long blonde beard when invention fails him, as it does every quarter of an hour. For a brilliant remark he says, " Haw, aw; just so," and twirls the ends of his moustache.

In the course of the evening they reach Paris, Madame's friend repairs to the Salle des Bagages, and after a struggle with the commissionnaires, secures a *fiacre* for her, and, radiant with success, announces that her luggage, including Thyrza's one box, is safely upon it. He inquires if there is anything further he can do for her, also where she is going to stay for the night. She gives him the address and laughingly bids him adieu. Thyrza cannot help speculating upon Miss Holt's probable remarks, could she behold Madame Dawson's free and easy manners.

It is eight o'clock in the evening. Crowds of people are sauntering in the streets and on the Boulevards, enjoying the cool air after the warmth and business of the day ; crowds of people sit sipping coffee and smoking cigars outside the cafés ; crowds of carriages, omnibuses, every description of vehicle, cross and recross in every direction.

Madame Dawson directs the driver of the *fiacre* to an hotel, and after having some supper, Thyrza goes to bed and is soon fast asleep, too tired to dream of any of the sights she has seen since the morning.

The steamer—" warranted A1, fast sailing, fitted up with every luxury and accommodation for the passengers "—which in much the above terms is advertised to cross the Channel from Calais to Dover, is nearly ready to start from the first-mentioned place.

Madame Dawson and Thyrza have triumphantly finished with the Custom House officers, who have found no contraband goods in either of their trunks, and they have now gone on deck, from whence they look on at the animated scene around them. It is not a bad study for those in search of character. Numbers of half-pay officers, persons who, owing to " circumstances over which they have no control," are obliged to reside abroad, seedy individuals who live by their wits, flash men who make money on the principle of the celebrated apophthegm, " Surely those with plenty of money and no brains was made for them with plenty brains and no money," lounge lazily on the quay, bent on nothing in particular, having merely come down out of curiosity to read the morning paper or watch the boat go off. Piles of luggage are being hauled on board, cabs heavily laden drive frantically up at the last moment, containing elderly ladies with lap-dogs and bandboxes, who speedily become a prey to extortionate porters. Patient paterfamilias, who has been taking his wife and family abroad on a small trip, stands, spectacles on nose, counting over dozens of packages, without which his woman-kind insisted life and the table d'hôte would have been a howling wilderness and desert unto them. A young artist, tall, pale, and dark, with eyes of true southern splendour, very baggy clothes and a slouch hat, in which he looks an embryo brigand, watches a couple of frizzy-haired girls, who are swearing vows of eternal fidelity, to be broken within a month. A Belgian family—four brothers, all short, all fat, and all wearing long chevelure and spectacles, accompanied by their two sisters—take possession of a seat near Madame and Thyrza. They are going to "do" Scotland; are got up in flaring tartan, have a notion that nothing is drunk in Scotland but whisky, nothing eaten but oatcakes and sheepshead, and haggis. They speak English imperfectly, and their invariable remark upon the surrounding scenery, pronounced slowly and with a slight lisp, is, " Very beautiful." An elderly lady, with a troop of small children like so many steps, comes up the companion-ladder on to the deck, in the most remote nook of which two lovers are evidently saying what is to be a long farewell. They are far too much occupied with each other to care what people are thinking about them. A gentleman, in a light grey overcoat and grey wide-awake hat, after lingering on the quay to hear the result of the races, saunters leisurely past Thyrza. Madame Dawson has hurriedly resumed her veil and gone down abruptly to the ladies' cabin, leaving Thyrza alone. Very solitary she looks, sitting by herself, her long dark hair hanging in thick tresses below her waist, a sort of dreamy *hunted* expression in the soft hazel eyes. She has on an old plaid cloak that has done duty as a wrap for Miss Holt during wet weather for the last dozen years; originally it was a Royal Stuart tartan, but the tints are faded and reduced to a wholly indescribable neutral hue, and the texture is worn and threadbare. Thyrza is aware of something queer about the brown straw hat, of a shape quite out of fashion, and a difference in the make and *tout ensemble* of her apparel, from that of the be-flounced, be-trimmed, be-frilled young girls on board. The cotton gloves that she only wears on Sundays when going to church at Villios, have been darned several times at the tips; and the strong, thick boots, made by a shoemaker accustomed to the construction of sabots for the peasantry in Villios, are admirably adapted for the stiff clay roads in that neighbournood, which after a shower of rain are transmogrified into mud, ankle deep, but not very well fitted for the respectable, civilized society in which she now finds herself.

Mr. Ferrier contemplates Thyrza's little lonely figure; there appears no one to speak to, or take any interest in her; and, finally, he advances towards her.

"Same old story everywhere, Mademoiselle Thyrza!" he says, after he has related his experience of Villios.

" How, Monsieur ?' '

" The old, old story, as sentimental people call it, of *spoonifying* and *humbugging* and *making love*. Look at that interesting pair who have just come on board; they are returning after the *treacle moon*. The man looks as if he has had enough of it. I know I should too with her. I should not think that beyond dress and millinery she had two ideas in her head."

" Oh, I thought she was so pretty ! and her dress is such a charming shade of blue," looking at her own dingy grey linen.

" Pretty doll, I grant you," continues Mr. Ferrier, glancing Thyrza slowly over from the crown of her brown straw hat until his eyes fix themselves on a patch that the local shoemaker has placed conspicuously on the very front of her boot. She tucks it out of sight as well as she can under her short dress, which she begins to think, though convenient for the purpose of climbing the apple-tree at the *pension*, or scrambling up the broken-down wall between Miss Holt's garden and her friend's, M. Joachim, the wine merchant next door, might advantageously be a little longer.

"She is pretty now, with the devil's own beauty—youth. But by the time she is forty, what an inane fool she will be! Poor fellow! Her husband will have a hard time of it. If he omits saying something sweet, she will be in a bad temper—pouting and weeping. I hate a crying woman. But after one has got to '*darling*' and '*angel*,' what *can* a fellow say? The height of adoration can go no further. There should be a new dictionary of fresh terms invented for the benefit of unfortunates undergoing the honeymoon, for it comes uncommon hard lines on a fellow to be in a continual state of invention. It would wear me out."

"The object of your pity looks as if he would manage to survive very well. I should not think he is much troubled with brains or imagination. We travelled with him yesterday from Rougeville to Paris," replies Thyrza, laughing at the recollection of the broad and open compliments Mr. Harris paid Madame Dawson. Young Mrs. Harris, if she knew it, would probably hardly smile so sweetly on her handsome, prosperous husband. "But where can Madame have gone?"

"The tall stout person in the green gown?"

"Yes. I am going with her to London. She is called Madame Dawson."

"Thanks for the information.   I fancy she has gone down into the saloon.   What makes her always wear a thick black veil?"

"She did not have it on when we came on board."

"Did she not?   Oh, she was putting it on in no end of a hurry when I walked on deck, and made off down the companion ladder at such a rate that I thought she must certainly come a cropper with those fine high-heeled boots of hers."

"I wish you could have seen her without the veil!   She is lovely—intensely beautiful."

"What strong adjectives you use—I suppose schoolgirls   always   do — 'lovely,' 'charming *et cetera!*'   Where are you going to?"

"I want to see why Madame has gone away. She will perhaps think it rude of me to stay here and leave her by herself."

"Never mind what she thinks—what does it matter?   She is probably sea-sick.   Although I should scarcely think she has had time to feel ill. Are you a good sailor?"

"I don't know.   It is twelve years since I was in a steamer."

"You don't mean to say you remember twelve years ago!"

"Well, not very clearly.   But I do in a sort of way."

"Not very distinctly, I should think. Now for an affecting farewell. Time's up."

Paterfamilias assures his anxious better half that the thirty odd boxes are safe; the lovers, with a tremendous effort, say good-bye.

"Don't watch the vessel out of sight, or we shall never meet again," she sobs.

"My own. Good-bye!"

"And you'll send me a telegram and write directly and tell me everything," she says for the hundredth time.

"Now, sir!" the Captain interferes.

"Good-bye, darling; remember 9 A.M. I *must* go. Good-bye!"

He moves away. She sinks down on the seat, covers her head in her shawl, and cries like any child.

"I wonder how many deluded beings have said the same words, and travelled over the same well-worn track," remarks Mr. Ferrier.

"But it is all fresh and new to them, poor things! I do hope they will meet again," says Thyrza, with genuine interest.

"I trust you are not going to join your tears to hers, just out of pure sympathy. Why, you don't imagine they will be faithful? The hotter their supposed affection is, the sooner it will burn itself out."

" Of course they will."

" Now, I'll tell you exactly what *he* will do. *He* will look at the boat going out of harbour and feel a little sentimental. Then he will take out his watch to see how long it will be before dinner, smoke a pipe, and think a B.-and-S. not a bad idea."

" What is a B.-and-S. ?"

" A B.-and-S. is a bottle of soda water with some brandy added to flavour it, and to take off the chill. It is convenient to call it B.-and-S. Brevity is the soul of wit. Now to finish the proceedings of *him*. After the B.-and-S., he will moon about, and, feeling dull in the evening, will pay a visit to a friend who has some lively daughters warmly attached to *her*, with whom he will amuse himself, merely to keep up his spirits, with a little flirtation. On the evening that *he* does not drop in at his friend's, *he* may patronize the billiard table. On the whole, *he* contrives to rub along pretty well. Man is a sociable animal, and was never meant to dwell in solitude by himself within four walls."

" And how about *her ?*"

" *She* will look disconsolate, as you see her now, for a few hours; but a glance at the mirror will convince her that crying is a bad speculation and will damage her chances. So she cheers up, sighs occasionally, talks volumes of rubbish to her confidante about ' darling ' *Blank* for a few days; is introduced to an eligible; makes herself agreeable to him."

" I don't believe it."

" After a time *he*, on the other side of the Channel, receives a short letter, which he stuffs into the hottest part of the fire. *She* has determined to wait no longer, and to go through life with the eligible."

" What a shame !"

" Not at all. There are as good fish in the sea as ever came out of it. *She* is a sensible young person not to wait for the chance of— as *he* phrases it—something turning up."

" What will become of *him ?*"

" *He* laments to his friends how badly he has been treated; thinks seriously of the next world for a short period, and the tailor's account he ought to square; discovers his mental misery does not afflict his appetite nor his digestive organs; reflects that his unhappiness will be lightened if shared; proposes eventually to some one who has only just appeared on the scene of action; marries her; meets the first *she* with calmness."

" *He* ought not to get over it so soon."

" Men die of many diseases, but I never knew

of any one who died of love or from a broken heart. You may depend people are tougher than that. Time blunts the feelings and reconciles one to everything. Why, it is beginning to rain!"

"Do you think we shall have a bad passage?"

"It looks queer and uncertain. In squally weather the boat is sometimes many hours in crossing. If you will allow me to arrange my rug for you, I think I can make you as comfortable as you would be below."

"I have nothing on that the rain can hurt," replies Thyrza, hesitating to open the rusty cotton Mrs. Gamp umbrella, filled with holes—a present from Miss Holt in a fit of extraordinary generosity at the last moment. Thyrza would rather be drenched through and through than be forced to let Mr. Ferrier see these disreputable holes and rags. She is not ashamed of the poverty and plainness of her dress, but she *is* ashamed of the tattered umbrella.

"True," says Mr. Ferrier; "and you have no complexion to wash off. But you may catch cold."

"I never catch cold."

"So much the better then," unfolding a tiger-skin rug, lined with scarlet, which he wraps round Thyrza, and opening a large white umbrella he sits down beside her. There is a stiff breeze blowing and a heavy swell on the waters; the boat ploughs her way with difficulty through the waves; the spray flies high, washing right on to the deck; the wet wind dashes salt racy tears in Thyrza's face, rendering her cheeks rosy like a crimson clove carnation; her hair glistens with raindrops, her eyes sparkle with animation; she can feel the engines leap beneath her as they struggle against a strong sou'-wester and the wild surf, and she exclaims—

"Oh, this is delicious !"

"You are not frightened then ?"

"Not a bit. And what splendid waves! There is a great black-green monster !" as the steamer sinks in the trough of one billow, then rises like a bird on the top of the next.

"Thought you would get on to 'splendid,' and so forth, sooner or later."

"You laugh at me."

"No; I was thinking you were a study. You know I am a *disagreeable* man. You thought so; come, do not deny it. I saw it plainly written on your countenance in the billiard-room. I suppose you threw away the rose out of the diligence window long before you got to Trois d'Or. Have you any objection to a cigar ?"

"No; I think it must be nice to smoke. I once took a whiff from old Mr. Spindler's pipe; but I thought I should have died, I was so ill afterwards."

"Ah! only want the opportunity, not the will, to be fast. Opportunity is everything. How neatly you have got out of it about the rose!"

Thyrza produces the rose from an envelope in her pocket.

"I apologize," says Mr. Ferrier; "I always make a point of doing so when I am in the wrong. Now, Mademoiselle, do you think you can hold the umbrella with both hands for a minute while I strike a light? Don't let it blow overboard; I have a sincere attachment to this umbrella, and also to my old wideawake hat. They have both been with me half over the world."

Only a few passengers remain on deck, most of them having gone below; for the rain is pouring as though it had never rained since the Deluge. The wind increases in strength, and they make but little progress against the combined elements. Owing to these circumstances, a nervous lady is certain they are all going to the bottom forthwith, and she is very indignant with her husband for refusing to remonstrate with the Captain. Nothing will induce her to quit her husband's arm, or to believe his assurance there is no danger. The artist stretches himself at full length on a rug. Wrapped up in a waterproof mackintosh and hat, he is independent of the weather, and fraternizes with a burly, close-shaven priest. A lanky American, fresh from the prairies of the far West, who has come to have a look at the little island of Britain, strides across to Ferrier's corner and settles himself near Thyrza.

"Guess it's going to be a dirty day," he observes.

"I daresay you are right," returns Ferrier.

"Been to Paris? So have I. Been taking out a patent for a new machine, which at the same time will cut, rake, bind in sheaves, and thresh. Ah!" slapping his knee emphatically, "with all your old family and blue blood in Britain, you can't buy brains."

"No, not in that way. But you can purchase their service. There is not much you cannot buy for money, and few circumstances that cannot, at least, be ameliorated by money. Everything has its price."

"Glad to hear you agree with me. Knew you were a man of sense. Been out of Britain before?"

" Yes."

" Bet any odds you like that you are a Scotchman. They are as long-headed and nearly as 'cute as we are. Yes. I told you so. Would have laid any stakes on it."

" How did you know ?"

" You are so deuced slow and calculating in your answers. An Englishman always says plump out yes or no, without hesitation. A Scotchman always stops a bit before he speaks for fear of committing himself; and is so cautious, you can only screw the whole truth out of him by a roundabout way. That is the reason the Scotch never say *Amen* at the end of their prayers. They are afraid of committing themselves to the minister's words."

Mr. Ferrier laughs.

" I suppose I may call myself a Scotchman. My father was a Scotchman, but my mother is English. When I was at home we lived in England. And before going to Scotland I shall run down to the old place for a few days to look up the old neighbourhood."

" Not resided in Scotland at all ?" asked the Yankee.

" Not yet; however, I hope soon to see the land of my ancestors. I feel quite a stranger in

Europe, as for the last eleven years I have been in China."

" Been in business ?"

Ferrier nods his head in affirmation.

" Tidy sort of business to be done there, I hear. Opium ?"

" There is no opium trade excepting what is done by smugglers."

" Going back ?"

" Yes ; in the course of a year. I shall return by the Pacific Railway and San Francisco. I should have been in England long ago if the steamer in which I sailed from Shanghai had not been obliged to put into Bombay for six weeks while repairs were being made to her engines."

" Splendid trip that from New York ! Well," his glance falling on Thyrza, " taking your *darter* home from school in Paris, I guess."

Mr. Ferrier and she look at each other, and burst out laughing simultaneously.

" I must confess, Mademoiselle Thyrza," says he.

" Rutherfurd," she suggests.

" Miss Rutherfurd, then. *My* name is Jack Ferrier. Well, I must confess I do *not* see much resemblance between my handsome visage and Mademoiselle's. She must be extremely flattered. I daresay I don't look over and above juvenile," taking off his hat and exhibiting to view a crop of thick black hair, considerably streaked with grey, " and old enough to be your father. Only it is rather a joke to be taken for the head of a family before one has hanged one-self in the fatal matrimonial noose. How old are you, Mademoiselle ? Fourteen or fifteen, at the outside ? You need not be ashamed yet of telling your age."

" I am seventeen past, Monsieur."

" Should not have thought it. You are small for your time of life; but probably you will grow."

" Beg pardon, sir," says the Yankee. " Had no idea but that you were the young lady's father. Made sure you were taking her from school. Meant no offence."

Ferrier intimates he understands nothing of the kind was intended.

" Going down to the cabin ?" continues the Yankee ; " can recommend the provisions as par-ticularly good."

Cousin Jonathan departs to obtain somewhat wherewith to refresh his inner man, saying some-thing to himself to the effect that there is " a considerable deal of human natur in a man when he sees a likely girl like that, and he reckons he has put his foot into it pretty well with that party." Ferrier and Thyrza are silent for some minutes. Then he speaks.

"A penny for your thoughts, Mademoiselle?"

"Will you pay the penny if I tell you?"

"How mercenary you are! Do not you give anything for nothing? Are you mentally comparing our supposed resemblance? You pass your hand over your chin as though you already felt the stubble of a beard growing."

"No, Monsieur. I was not thinking of you at all."

"Of whom, or of what, then?"

"I was wondering what Mr. Spindler would be doing at this time in the *pension*, and how the Italian is getting on."

"I don't know about Mr. Spindler, but I can tell you of the lad. Mr. Spindler called upon me after you had driven off with Madame Dawson in the diligence. We talked over matters. I found him a much more rational being than I had anticipated."

"Poor Mr. Spindler!" says Thyrza. "Cannot any one be considered to have common sense unless he has been in business?"

"Business is by no means to be despised; especially if it *pays*. I don't say there are not higher things in the world. That is not the question," returned Ferrier. "Well, after a long consultation, Mr. Spindler and myself got the boy apprenticed to a tailor in Villios."

"Oh, Monsieur; how droll! A tailor of all people in the world."

"The first thing we did was to have his hair cut, and a new suit of clothes provided for him. He was not such a suitable object for a picture as when he presented himself before the window of your *pension*, but he has a chance of being immeasurably better than artistic—a well-behaved member of society. On the whole it was a good thing he happened to fall and cut his head. Are you hungry?"

"Desperately," says Thyrza, concisely.

"So am I. Shall we follow our Brother Jonathan's example, and discover what sort of sustenance is provided for the wayfarer?"

"I daresay Madame Dawson will be glad to see me."

"Madame Dawson? I think somehow I've seen that woman before. Are you going to live with her in London?"

"No. I am only travelling with her. I go on to-morrow morning to a place called Lillies-hill, in Kilniddryshire, in Scotland."

"Lillieshill! Why, who the deuce do you know there?"

"I don't know any one—I wish I did. At least, I *have* seen Mr. Mark. But one does not remember much at the advanced age of five years."

"Mark? Why!" exclaims Ferrier, looking exceedingly perplexed.

"I am going to Lillieshill by Mr. Mark's own special invitation," replies Thyrza. "Are *you* Mr. Mark?"

"No, of course not. Did I not tell you my name was Ferrier? But I see it now. You are the little girl whose father and mother died at Shanghai, and whom Mark has been looking after."

"Yes," Thyrza answers, "you are right. But how do you know Mr. Mark?" she asks in her turn.

"Mark is the greatest friend I have. We were in partnership in Shanghai. He has given up business now, and come home for altogether. I have got a new partner, a fellow called Lennox. But the idea of Mark being guardian to a girl like you!"

"He is not my guardian."

"Well, well; comes to the same thing in the end. He acts the part without the name."

"I suppose Mr. Mark is a benevolent stout man, rather bald, and not tall?"

"Mark *would* be pleased to hear your opinion. However, you will see him for yourself this time to-morrow evening."

"My ideas are most probably all wrong," says Thyrza.   "Madame——"

"Oh, hang Madame!" breaks in Ferrier. "Excuse me, Mademoiselle; that slipped out unawares. I have been living for the last five years up the Yang-tse-Kiang, about a hundred and fifty miles from Shanghai, and have scarcely spoken to a woman during that time, so I am afraid my manners have deserted me. Depend upon it, Madame has never given you a thought. She has hung up that marvellous yellow hair to save it from being crushed, and is at this moment lying flat upon her back in her berth as ill as possible, and groaning in despair. Odd! I can't get it out of my head, there is something familiar about her."

"You cannot have seen her before. She is an Andalusian, and married an English artist. She lived, until last year, in a flat in the Quartier Latin, when her husband died just as he came into an immense fortune."

"Queer," says Mr. Ferrier, doubtfully. "When did you first see her?"

"We were introduced in the diligence at Villios."

" And she told you her history at once, without knowing anything about you."

" Yes, she did."

" Hum ! Well, there are the white cliffs of Dover. We shall be in directly. What a shower ! Are you very wet ? Steady, don't be afraid. Let us get into the saloon."

Mr. Ferrier is greeted by the Yankee, who looks approvingly at Thyrza. She passes on to the ladies' cabin, where Madame is sitting, no trace of sea-sickness about her.

" What a sly little puss you are !" says she. " That is generally the case with you demure demoiselles. You have been sitting on deck this long while with the stiff Englishman, and forgot about poor me alone here without a friend to speak to."

" Oh, no, Madame ; indeed I did not."

" And what did you talk about ? Ah, you never spoke of *me*."

" Various subjects, and *you* among the rest. Mr. Ferrier"—Thyrza may be mistaken, but she cannot refrain from thinking Madame starts slightly and that the rose in her wax-like cheek fades—" Mr. Ferrier wondered why you always wore a black veil."

" It would not be proper for a desolate widow to travel without some sort of protection."

At this juncture the steward is heard announcing something in a loud voice in the saloon.

"We are just in," says Madame. She pins the black veil over her bonnet, and with the rest of the passengers hurries up on deck. The good ship steams along straight as an arrow shot from a tough ash bow over the swelling waves and tremendous surf. The white cliffs, crowned by the castle and fair green daisy-covered slopes, lying against a blue sky, come nearer. The rain has now ceased, and a rainbow stretches its arch of three colours across the sky, and Ferrier's lean bronzed face and keen eyes soften as if some strong emotion passed over them. Then come the crowd of cabbies and green-coated porters, and the sound of the familiar English tongue, and a Cockney pronouncing it is a warm day.

The Yankee consoles a doleful and sea-sick fellow-traveller, whom he assists to land, with—

" You should not have taken so much whisky to-day; I knew how it would be. You should fight against it, and resolve not to be sick, and make up your mind to keep well. It only wants *resolution*."

An original, if not a feasible idea. If one could remain in good health by merely willing it, there would be no employment for doctors, and, like the Wandering Jew, one might live on for ever. It may be recommended, however, as a new and cheap cure for sea-sickness which deserves consideration.

" You had better telegraph to let Mark know you have got all right to England," says Ferrier, when they have landed and are waiting for the important arrival of the boxes from the hold. " Or shall I send the telegram for you ?"

Thyrza gratefully accepts his offer. Madame has put up a parasol and turned her back upon Ferrier. Thyrza observes him giving sundry quick looks at her, but they must be very piercing indeed if they penetrate through the thickness of the shady veil and parasol. Madame is tongue-tied.

" I am sorry I cannot travel down with you, Mademoiselle," pursues Ferrier ; " but I shall be at Carmylie—that is, near Lillieshill—the end of next week. Tell Mark both I and his flask will put in an appearance then."

CHAPTER IV.

AN old house, built of red sandstone, half enshrined in ivy, with mullions and many nooks and corners, and overhanging eaves, and odd staircases leading nowhere in particular—a quaint house, to which the fancies of several generations of owners of different tastes have added a wing in one part, an entrance in another, blocking up doors and opening out windows in all manner of strange and unexpected places—a house which, in every sense of the words, shows traces of being lived in and cared for. This is Lillieshill. Like most old houses, it lies low, and is built on a flat piece of ground entirely shut in by trees. Near the house is located a thriving colony of rooks that are just now winging their way to their nests from a turnip-field, after a friendly discussion on things in general and grubs and worms in especial.

Through an opening in the trees, above a

artificial cascade falling into a pond with a miniature island in the centre;, glimpses of rugged purple mountain peaks are visible, dappled with tender lights and shades melting into soft, pearly distance; inky, indigo masses of pine forests embracing their feet; brown peat-tinged burns winding among the upland fields, winking gold in the sun; and green larches, their little scarlet tassel cones beginning to turn into dun colour.

Lillieshill is always pretty. In early spring, when the wind stirs the budding beech leaves putting their heads out of their ruddy shells; in summer, when they are interlacing their polished silver arms loaded with shimmering green foliage; in autumn, when the branches are decked with scarlet and yellow, turned into rubies by the shifting sunlight, and the red squirrels lay up stores of the russet beech mast; or in winter, when the powdered driven snow spreads its white garment on the earth—Lillieshill is always fair, but perhaps never fairer than as now, at the hour of sundown on an evening in May.

On the lawn, near the front door, is a group of three persons—a lady and two gentlemen. They are absorbed in the useful occupation of killing time, and are evidently expecting some one. Place aux dames.

Miss Lefroy is about fifty years of age, thin, wrinkled, and decidedly plain. No one in the pleasant, though now remote days of her youth, had ever called Miss Lefroy other than very moderately good-looking. Matrimonially speaking, she has been a failure. In other words, she is an old maid. She is not ashamed of the name, and is on the whole not discontented with her condition— *i.e.*, having plenty of money and little to employ her time. In spite of a certain stiffness and reserve in her manner, she is warmhearted and charitable, as the poor round Lillieshill and in the town of Queensmuir will testify. As her own hopes regarding herself have not come to fruition, Miss Lefroy hopes much for Mark. A woman, as a rule, must hope, if not for herself, for some one else. What she trusted would have been her own destiny she trusts will be realized in her favourite nephew, Mark. She is an accomplished linguist, and an earnest reader of the "Antiquity of Man," and puzzles her brain with "The Origin of Species," the cosmic vapour, and other abstruse subjects; but no one meeting her in society would guess that her abilities were above the ordinary run. Although an old maid, she has not imbibed the Woman's Rights mania, nor has she arrived at the pitch of spelling that word with a capital letter; neither has she the least desire to expatiate on a platform in public, under the impression she is born to set the world as it ought to be, and remedy the grievances of society. In Mr. Lefroy she has great faith. She believes with him that he is the handsomest as well as the most talented and most fascinating of men, which says a good deal for both brother and sister, a prophet not being without honour save in his own country.

Miss Lefroy's opinion of her brother is scarcely shared by Luke Mark, a young man of two or three and thirty, lately returned from China. He often finds Mr. Lefroy prosy and dull, especially as he does not take the same interest in prize cattle and old china and model cow-houses and dairies as Mr. Lefroy does. In appearance, Luke Mark is much what he was as a boy. He has blue eyes, fair hair, and a hooked nose, and he wears a blonde moustache. He is about five feet eight and a half in height, and there is an inexpressible air of neatness and dapperness about his whole outer man.

Mr. and Miss Lefroy wish their nephew to marry. They are the sole survivors of a large family, and the next heir after Mark is a shopkeeper in the West End of London, who, being poor in his early days, had been glad to put his pride in his pocket, and work as a shopboy until better times came. These better times, as far as money was concerned, have already come round, and still more prosperous ones are in store for him, if Mark remains unmarried. The notion of a man who had worn a white apron and stood behind a counter becoming the possessor of Lillieshill, its curiosities, its fat lands, its superb cattle, its splendid hothouses and appurtenances, is not pleasing to the Lefroys. Mr. Lefroy feels that if such comes to pass, he will not be able to lie peacefully in his grave. Such a man could not possibly appreciate the merits of old Dresden and Sèvres; and as for the precious cattle, the apple of his eye and the joy of his soul, the only charm the next heir would see in them would be their capability of being converted into beef and money. This is an agonizing idea to their affectionate owner.

So Mr. and Miss Lefroy, with the knowledge they cannot live for ever, and must, some time or other, quit Lillieshill for the narrow resting-place in their family burial ground at Queensmuir, earnestly desire that Mark should marry.

As for Mr. Lefroy, he is a very particular and fussy elderly man with the relics of former good looks still remaining. He carries his peculiarities to such an extent, that he has doormats for ornaments in the hall, and others which are intended to serve their normal purpose of removing the mud from the boots or shoes of visitors, and special stands for sticks; also, separate ones for umbrellas. In winter, he carefully airs his hat and gloves before the stove fire, to prevent all danger of catching cold. Everything about Lillieshill is sure to be "his own idea," or else "his own invention," and everything belonging to him is the finest of its kind. When he gets into the next world, he will miss his turtle-soup and his prize cattle, unless some very material change comes to his feelings before then.

"By-the-bye, when do the people come to dinner?" asks Mark.

"Half-past seven," returns Miss Lefroy.

"Any one worth speaking to?"

"Mrs. Ferrier from Carmylie, your partner's mother, and her married daughter, Mrs. Napier. Husband a Captain in the Rifle Brigade in India. But you know all about them, as you have seen them before."

"Well."

"The MacNabs from Quentinshope."

"Who are they?"

"Rich retired jute merchants."

"Oh!"

"My dear fellow, they are as rich as Crœsus—could eat gold if they liked," breaks in Mr. Lefroy.

"I daresay. Usual style of thing, I suppose. Rose from being a shoeblack, or something of the kind, with sixpence in his pocket."

"No; MacNab was not a shoeblack," responds Mr. Lefroy. "His father was a weaver and his mother a cook. MacNab himself began life as a clerk, and fortune favoured him. He has had a capital education, and is a shrewd, clever man."

"I don't doubt it."

"It is useless to ignore these sort of people, Luke, for there the fact is. They are the great power of the age. MacNab is a good sort of fellow; he behaves himself; he does not talk shop. If you had not been told you would never have guessed his mother was a cook. And a very excellent cook too," proceeds Mr. Lefroy, rubbing his hands; "I remember her perfectly well at Carmylie, many years ago now, when the Campbells owned the place."

"From whom the Ferriers bought it."

"Yes; the Campbells went to smash, and old Ferrier bought the place dirt cheap. Bless me! People don't ask *how* did you make your money? It is, how much has he got? Or, has he got any at all?"

" Well, now for the elegant French girl," says Luke Mark. " Grecian bend, Roman fall, and two or three pounds' worth of hair that grew on somebody else's head."

" I hope she does not wear nails in her boots," rejoins Mr. Lefroy, reflectively. " I should not like to have the new oak in the library scratched."

" She must stay at least three weeks, I suppose," sighs Miss Lefroy. " Whatever shall we do with a fashionable young lady at Lillies-hill, and more especially one accustomed to live in a town ? She is your visitor, Luke, not mine ; so you must look after her. There are the horses, at any rate ; so you can ride and drive with her, and we may get up a pic-nic or two."

" Perhaps she takes an interest in cattle or old china. If so, there will be always the model cowhouse and the old Dresden for her to amuse herself with," says Mr. Lefroy. " Oh ! sweet effect there !" pointing to a gleam of sunshine stealing through the russet-hued beech buds from which the green leaves are bursting, and the long drooping branches that touch the smooth sward.

" There she is !" cries Miss Lefroy, as a carriage drives along the gravel sweep to the house.

It does not enter into Thyrza's head to wait until she is assisted to descend. Directly the carriage stops she springs out to the gravel walk, to the astonishment of the stately footman, who announces that Mr. and Miss Lefroy and Mr. Mark are at home in a voice of displeasure at her unconventional proceedings.

Mark and his uncle and aunt are so amazed at the advent of the childish figure dressed in such odd, clumsy clothes, that at first they think there must be some mistake, and remain silent, until at last Mark gives vent to a lengthy " Whe-ew !"

Thyrza walks forward to meet them, ignorant of their feelings of astonishment. Her hat-string has broken on the journey, and it has fallen off in leaving the carriage. She picks it up and comes along with it in her hand, through the bright sunshine, her hair blowing about over her shoulders.

" Please, I have not come to the wrong house, have I ?" she asks, terrified at no one speaking, and clutching nervously to the Mrs. Gamp umbrella, which has clung faithfully to her during all her travels. No one ever loses an old gingham. It is always a nice new dapper silk one that evaporates and is never heard of again. " Please, I'm Thyrza Rutherfurd."

"To be sure!" exclaims Mark, heartily. "Welcome to Lillieshill, Miss Rutherfurd. Glad you have found your way safely. Troublesome long journey. I hear you met my friend Ferrier; I had a note from him this morning telling me about you."

"You must be very tired, dear," says Miss Lefroy, her mind infinitely relieved from the idea of the Girl of the Period she imagined she would be cooped up with for several weeks; and her heart goes out to the pale and somewhat weary face.

"A little, thank you," replies Thyrza, with a strong French accent.

"We expected a regular boarding-school young lady," pursues Mark, in explanation of his hesitation in welcoming her, which has clearly left a painful impression on her mind; "it is a long time since you and I met, so you must excuse me if at first I did not quite remember your features."

"You are Mr. Mark?" she inquires.

"Yes; at least I believe so. I trust no claimant will arrive to assert he is Luke Mark, and that I am somebody else."

"Then it is you who are my benefactor," she replies. "I give you my best thanks for all your kindness to me."

She says it as if instructed what words to use,

and her manner puts Mark on his most courteous behaviour.

"I am well repaid, Miss Rutherfurd, by having the pleasure of seeing you here to-day," he answers, politely.

"How did you manage about changing for Queensmuir at Bogdrum Junction?" asks Mr. Lefroy. "I hope you had no trouble about your luggage?"

"Is that the place where a man calls out suddenly, 'Change hee-ar for Queensmuir,' just as if some one had run a pin into him?" she rejoins, with a merry laugh, which does away in great measure with any further formality.

"I suppose it must have been."

"Well, I asked for my box there, and the man with the abrupt squeaky voice said it was not in the van. So I have lost it."

"Lost it?—how unfortunate! Some people are coming to dinner, too, to-night. How will you manage without an evening dress?"

"Oh, I had no evening dresses in it, so it does not signify."

"Was it directed?"

"No, I don't think it was."

"Dear me, dear me!—very provoking, to be sure, for you! Most annoying—particularly so. Ought to telegraph at once to the station-master at Queensmuir. Case of gross neglect—culpable neglect of duty. Shall kick up a pretty row, and get some one punished," says Mr. Lefroy, beginning to walk up and down the lawn as if violently agitated.

" Was it labelled for Queensmuir?" asks Mark.

" La—belled?"

" Had it a pink or blue luggage-ticket put on it at King's Cross?"

" I do not know. There was such a crowd at the station, and everybody did seem in such a hurry I never saw it after it was taken from the cab."

" The chances are you will never see it again," returns Mark, consolingly. " As to kicking up a shindy with the Company, that's no use. You've no claim against them unless it was properly labelled and directed."

" Miss Rutherfurd, will you come into the drawing-room, and have a cup of tea?" says Miss Lefroy, with a smile; " then you can rest a little before dinner."

" Oh yes, I should like that, for I am *so* hot and sticky and uncomfortable. You see I have had so many misfortunes, and broken the string of my hat, and lost my gloves, besides my box," answers Thyrza, cordially.

"Purvis, bring some tea," to the tall footman.
" Sit down on the sofa, dear."

Thyrza leans back luxuriously, while Miss
Lefroy laments the loss of the box. Such a
deliciously cool room it is, furnished with walnut-
wood and hangings of different shades of green
from palest sea-green to the darkest moss-tint.
A scent as of pot pourri, or dried violets, lingers
in its recesses. The walls are hung with pictures by various choice masters both ancient and
modern ; the corners filled with cabinets inlaid
with gold and porcelain of great antiquity.

A conservatory, separated from the drawing-
room by a glass door, discloses arcades of the
clinging festoons of the Virginia creeper, which
will shortly be out in profusion ; New Zealand
ferns and small palm trees stand in large tubs in
rows up and down.

Tea appears presently on a tiny round tray.
Thyrza helps herself, and pours out cream from a
stumpy crystal jug, studded over with little knobs
of green and ruby.

" What a pretty place !" exclaims Thyrza,
attacking the thin slices of home-made bread
and butter with relish. " If only I had not lost
my box, I should be quite happy."

" Mr. Lefroy will see about it for you to-
morrow. I am afraid nothing can be done

to-day. Poor child!—I am so sorry for it," rejoins Miss Lefroy. "I know what it is to arrive at a strange place without any of my possessions."

Miss Lefroy's fingers long to smooth Thyrza's rough hair, and pin her collar straight for her. Thyrza's collars had always a knack of slipping towards the back of her neck, and her hats a strong inclination to remain in *any* position rather than in the proper one of straight on the top of her head. If a briar, or nail, or loose screw were anywhere at hand, her dress or petticoat never missed an opportunity of getting entangled, usually to its great and grievous detriment. Uncared for, with no one to mind whether she looked well or ill at the *pension*, she has grown up without any of the little arts and small vanities which most girls employ to embellish their persons. Continually told she was plain and ugly, she has hitherto thought it useless to take pains in adorning herself. Not that she has not thought about her appearance. Like the majority of girls, one of the dearest desires of her heart is to be pretty; and with the conviction of her own defects, she has an ardent admiration for the beautiful.

"I am afraid you must think I am a dreadfully untidy girl," says Thyrza, rising, and looking at herself in one of the numerous mirrors. "What a guy I am, and what a number of smuts have settled on the end of my nose!"

"People do look a little untidy after a long journey," returns Miss Lefroy, evasively.

"But, really, I am *sometimes* neat, though, in general, I am not a very tidy person."

"We must try to find some kind of a gown for you, my dear," pursues Miss Lefroy, taking Thyrza upstairs. "Luke brought a large box home from China with him, in which very likely we may discover a dress that will fit you."

She produces a bunch of keys, and after a considerable amount of fiddling and hackling at the lock with every key on the bunch before finding the right one, opens a big chest, on which are the initials "T. R." in brass-headed nails.

On the top lie sundry Chinese curiosities of wonderful embroidery on scarlet and black cloth, a bag filled with the ordinary coin of the Celestials, heavy and inconvenient as to size and weight; a collection of beautifully-carved ivory idols and odd figures engaged in wrestling, and specimens of the red, white, and yellow balls worn by the different grades of Mandarins. Below are dresses of a fashion long since out of date, skimpy in the skirts, and peculiar about the body and sleeves. There is nothing that Thyrza can wear.

"Oh, who is this?" she cries abruptly, pulling out a water-colour sketch of a woman's head, painted on a rough piece of sketching-paper.

"I have not the slightest idea," says Miss Lefroy; "I daresay Luke knows. But most probably it is merely a fancy head. Put it into one of these drawers, and then you will find it when you want it again. 'A place for everything and everything in its place' is a valuable maxim. Come to my room, and we will see if any of my gowns could be converted into a garment for you. No, I fear not."

Rumbles of carriage-wheels are now audible on the sweep, and young ladies with fans and opera-cloaks begin to alight.

"What shall we do?" exclaims Miss Lefroy. "There is no gown that will fit you. Ah! I know."

She turns in the collar of Thyrza's little grey linen dress, pins broad, rich white lace round the opening, fastens black velvet and a pearl brocch at her throat, combs her thick hair back from her forehead, tying it with red ribbons; and taking a spray of scarlet geraniums and maiden-hair fern from a vase, places it on one side of her head.

"What do you think of yourself now?" she asks.

"Oh, how nice I look! Really just like other

people.   Thank you ever so much," throwing her arms round Miss Lefroy's neck, not to the benefit of the neat arrangement of her cap.   She is not accustomed to being embraced—indeed very few persons would have had the hardihood even to dream of embracing her—and she is, in consequence, surprised and a little taken aback at Thyrza's open expression of pleasure.

" I say!" exclaims a voice outside Miss Lefroy's bedroom door.

" Yes, Richard."

" I say, Fan."

" Yes, Richard," responds Miss Lefroy, going to the door, and opening it.

" What!—are not you dressed yet?   Nearly everybody has come, and cook has sent word that if she does not dish up at once the dinner will be spoilt ; and after the trouble I have taken about arranging the menu, that would be very disappointing.   It might give me a fit of indigestion, and probably—most probably—would cause me a sleepless night."

" I will be as quick as I can," returns Miss Lefroy.   " Miss Rutherfurd, would not you like to go down with Mr. Lefroy ?"

" Oh no, thank you," says Thyrza.   " I had rather wait for you."

" My maid has gone for her holiday just now,"

proceeds Miss Lefroy, putting on a violet-silk gown and a cap to match, with violets and white marabout feathers. "Here is my dressing-case, dear. Will you choose some rings or bracelets for me? I am so pleased I have managed so nicely about your frock. I know girls think so much about their appearance. I used also when I was your age. Let me see : you want a sash yet, and a pair of lace sleeves to finish you. Did not Miss Holt give you enough to eat? You are not very fat."

"Oh yes : Miss Holt was not quite so bad as all that. We had always plenty of food."

"I never was at school myself—horrid places, I think. Invariably, some black sheep there. About gloves : you ought to have a pair—these are rather soiled."

"I can carry them in my hand to show I have some," says Thyrza—a bright idea striking her. She holds up for Miss Lefroy's selection a big emerald, like a lump of green fire, on a band of gold without any of the metal round the stone, and a hoop of coral and brilliants.

"Very well, dear," answers Miss Lefroy, drawing on the rings, and settling her spectacles on her nose.

They go down to the drawing-room, and after a few remarks upon the inexhaustible and prevailing topic of the weather, the guests pair off into dinner, Thyrza falling to the lot of a very tall young man, blessed with a prodigious opinion of himself and a wide expanse of shirt-front. He is the eldest hope of the MacNab family; and will, on the decease of his father, inherit an immense fortune. In course of time he intends marrying, but not one of the Kilniddryshire girls. They are not fine enough for him. Nothing under an Earl's daughter will suit the heir of Quentinshope. He lives in daily apprehension of some one " hooking him," and regards the majority of women as so many mantraps set to ensnare his valuable self.

At first he seems inclined to be friendly with Thyrza, and imagining she is of French extraction from her foreign accent and appearance, he tries to air his French ; but observing a twinkle of fun in her eyes on his saying something about " avec très beaucoup distingué plaisir," which answer of his to a question of Thyrza's unfortunately occurs at one of those dead silences which sometimes happen in the conversation at a party, he abandons any further attempts at talking for the more substantial delights of the table.

The dinner and its appointments are perfect. Mr. Lefroy devotes most of his spare time to the study of the science of cookery, which he regards

as an art. " God sends good food" is a favourite
quotation of his, " but the devil makes the cooks."
What he is going to have for dinner is his first
thought in the morning; how it will turn out
oppresses him towards evening, and when the
suspense is over, and he finds the fish boiled to
the requisite firmness, he subsides into a condition
of placid good temper. The certain way to get
on with Mr. Lefroy is to flatter him. Carping
critics of John Stuart Mill's life have declared the
reason he idolized his wife and entertained so
high an opinion of her intellect, was because she
knew how to flatter his weak points. One very
weak point of Mr. Lefroy's is his great capacity
for swallowing any amount of flattery, no matter
how gross and palpable; and any one aware of
this quality might lead him very easily.

He has taken some trouble in arranging the
party, which consists of himself, Miss Lefroy,
Thyrza, Luke Mark, Mr. and Mrs. MacNab of
Quentinshope, Archibald MacNab younger, and
his two sisters, Lola and Jane—tall, dashing
girls, with freckled complexions and pale hair;
Mrs. Napier, known as the White Witch in her
husband's regiment; Mr. Dods, the minister of
Carmylie fishing village; Mr. Hislop, the bank
agent for the British Jute Company in Queensmuir, the neighbouring post town; and Lord and

Lady George Bogg, an old married couple, who, during forty years of wedded life, have grown singularly like each other, the only apparent difference being that Lord George has a beard, and wears a coat and trousers, and Lady George has no beard, and is dressed in ordinary woman's guise. The whole party are comfortably accommodated at one of those pleasant round tables where you are not separated from your opposite neighbour by a desert of tablecloth, but may converse with him or her, as the case may be, without requiring to raise your voice to an alarming pitch.

Dinners by daylight are never so successful as those by gas or candlelight. The sun is not merciful to faded complexions, and exposes any attempt to "make up" with unsparing severity. The ladies' jewels do not sparkle properly, and even Lady George's diamond necklace, and the star in the false plait over her wrinkled forehead, lose half their brilliancy. Neither does the silver and crystal on the table look so bright as it does in the winter evenings when the shutters are closed, the crimson curtains drawn across the French windows, a fire burns on the old-fashioned brass dogs, that have not been abolished from Lillieshill, and a good lamp sheds its soft light over the gilt picture-frames and the pretty gowns of the guests. Conversation does not flow so freely either. Bon mots and jeux d'esprit sound poor; it is, in fact, like talking sentiment at breakfast in the glare of broad daylight. Then one feels rather guilty at devoting so much time to dining when without all is so fresh and sweet, and that most charming hour of the summer day, the twilight, comes on. When the sun has set, and there is that momentary hush and stillness in the air just before night fairly falls, and a bird chirps to its mate among the ivy at Lillieshill, one wishes to stroll out through the rose-garden, and loiter a little in the long avenue of stately lime-trees, instead of sitting down to a formal dinner.

Mr. Lefroy infinitely prefers dining by candle-light, but Miss Lefroy has persuaded him not to exclude the day. So the sun is permitted to shine its last rays through the beeches into the dining-room, and although it does not set off Lady George's diamonds to their usual advantage, it would be hard to find fault with the golden beams that trickle over the tree-tops and settle on Mrs. Napier's fair hair. Nor indeed could much objection be found with the view of mountains, woods, fields, and the mossy lawn, the last mentioned one of the prides and beauties of Lillieshill.

" Nothing in the papers at present, excepting the usual amount of accidents and the wonderful Tichborne trial," observes Luke Mark.

" There never is at this time of year; the chief place is occupied with the proceedings of Parliament," replies the elder Mr. MacNab. " How are your turnips looking, Mr. Lefroy ?"

" Oh, pretty well. We shall want rain before long. I am going to try a new kind of top-dressing of my own invention, on some fields on the Home Farm."

" How beautifully green the fields are about Lillieshill," says Lola MacNab.

" The result of irrigation on a plan of my own. If you want a thing done well, do it yourself."

" As *Punch* said when the master of the house got up shivering at 4 A.M. on a cold winter's morning to let in the chimney-sweep. Poor John Leech ! how inimitably he drew," rejoins Mark.

" Have you been long in this part of the globe ?" asks the minister, Thyrza's other neighbour.

" No, I only came to Lillieshill to-day."

" She lost her luggage at Bogdrum," adds Miss Lefroy.

" Ought to have your initials painted on your

boxes," breaks in Mr. Lefroy ; "I have mine—idea of my own. Initial L, as long as this, painted on black ground, known all over Scotland. See it even on the darkest night in that condemned criminal's cell at the Waverley Station, where you are forced to rout out your luggage on the way from the South. Scandalous shame, scandalous! Capital of Scotland, too. Never trust to railway guards—humbugs, delusions. Look after it yourself. Have particular covers or marks by which they can be identified, and take off the old labels when you get home, in case of mistake."

" There are wonderfully few cases of lost luggage, if you consider the enormous quantity of traffic and how hard-worked the servants of the Company are," says the minister.

" Partridges are likely to be scarce and small. The immense amount of rain we have had did them a great deal of harm."

" What sort of condition are the rivers in, Mr. Dods? You are the angler *par excellence* of this district."

" I have not been able to do much yet, the waters have been so muddy and swollen with the late heavy rains. But when the May fly is on the Bogg I anticipate some fair sport."

" Fishing always seems to me a cowardly and

cruel sport," says Lola MacNab; "fancy a great big man spending hours in enticing a poor little fish out of the water. There it lies with the hook in its mouth panting with pain."

"Fish were made to be eaten, Miss MacNab," remarks Mr. Lefroy, solemnly; "besides, they are cold-blooded creatures, and do not feel much."

"Indeed, Miss MacNab, I must own I have sometimes felt rather guilty, too, when I saw the trout lying on the bank looking up at me with its fine black eyes almost reproachfully. But as Mr. Lefroy says, they are intended to be eaten, and they have always a fair chance of escape. They need not bite unless they like."

This is the first dinner party at which Thyrza had ever been present. As time goes on, and course after course is removed, and entrée after entrée arrives and is handed round by the footmen, seeing no dishes on the table she becomes a good deal surprised. She waits patiently for the beef to appear and be placed on the table, but minutes elapse and still nothing comes, and the flowers and fruit alone ornament Mr. Lefroy's hospitable mahogany.

"Where is the rest of the dinner?" she at last inquires of the minister. "I don't see it in the room."

"We-el, Miss Rutherfurd," he rejoins, endeavouring unsuccessfully to modulate the loud, distinct tones of his voice, grown sonorous and bass from long practice in addressing sleepy congregations in the kirk at the fishing village, "we-el, it's on the side table, and this is called the dîner à la Russe. I am exactly of your opinion in this respect, and like to see what I am eating. The dîner à la Russe is very well if you are not hungry, for what with talking, and the constant changing of the plates, one does not get much to eat at a dinner party."

"Oh, do you think so?" answers Archie MacNab, having overheard the minister's observation, and speaking much in the tone in which the London swell, on hearing a country cousin had committed the enormity of eating mustard with mutton, exclaimed, "Did the fellow die?" "I never like to see a lady hewing away at a couple of tough chickens or a huge joint of underdone beef—there is something very revolting in the idea."

"Ice, Miss?" inquires the footman of Thyrza.

Slightly confused, she inadvertently places the useful cooling article intended for her champagne on her plate beside a rissole, which, being hot, presently melts it into a small pool of water. By this time she has recovered herself, and grows uncomfortably hot on perceiving her mistake. She hopes no one has observed it, but Archie MacNab calls out for the ice to be brought back and insists on putting it himself into her wine-glass. It has the effect of rendering Thyrza silent until the ladies leave the dining-room.

"Have you been attending the Parochial Board in Queensmuir lately, Mr. Lefroy?" asks the minister.

"Not for the last two months," rejoins Mr. Lefroy. "Perfect bear-garden, perfect bear-garden. The last time I was there I gave those presump-tuous, conceited fellows a bit of my mind, I can tell you. They are none the worse for being sworn at a little. In fact, without that they would argue you out of your Christian name. *I* soon said what *I* meant."

Just as Thyrza is speculating how much longer they will be at dinner—by the timepiece on the mantelpiece they have already been more than two hours and a half in the dining-room—Miss Lefroy gives a mysterious glance to the ladies, on which they rise in a body; silks, satins, and muslins rustle into the passage, leaving the lords of creation to their walnuts and wine.

The farewell flounce is scarcely conveyed in safety through the doorway, when Miss Lefroy begins to discuss the educational statistics of

Scotland with Mrs. MacNab. Lady George is too deaf to hear without her ear-trumpet, so rests content in a large armchair, and allows her dinner to digest. The educational statistics of Scotland and the School Board have no attractions for Mrs. MacNab. What she likes is to relate all the peccadilloes and misdoings of her servants during the last ten years, and to hear what wages are given by Mr. Lefroy and Lord George. Any other equally interesting domestic particulars are received by her with much relish. As for Lola and Jane MacNab, they are compelled to take refuge in looking over a number of pictures of Chinese scenery, brought home from Shanghai by Luke Mark. No man being in the room, Mrs. Napier does not trouble herself to open her pretty mouth. Napier's White Witch, as the men of the Rifle Brigade had called Charity in India, well deserves the sobriquet. Charming as a girl, she has developed into a still more charming woman. To a complexion white and pure as the snow on Monte Rosa, she adds the contrast of miraculously-pencilled dark eyebrows. Yet there is not a really good feature in her face. Her eyes are not large nor remarkable for beauty of expression or colour, still she contrives to make wonderful " play" with them ; her mouth is somewhat wide, but her lips are red as roses ; and no one looking at the fair, soft, babyish countenance, the silky, flaxen hair cut à la Vandyke over her forehead, and falling behind in a cascade of curls nearly to her waist, and the slim, tall, *svelte* figure —the admiration of every man and the envy of most of her own sex—could help saying, " What a sweet woman !"

She is very popular among men, and is as much admired in Kilniddryshire now she is a wife as she was when a girl at Blackbeck House; but she has anything but the love of women. Her manners are extremely pleasant, and she can talk on any subject from Colenso to bonnets, having a smattering of knowledge and " small talk " on the principal topics of the day. As she generally suits her conversation to the style of person to whom she is speaking, and has a peculiarly angelic way of giving forth her opinions as if asking for advice, it is not astonishing she should be a general favourite with men. Beyond herself, her dress, and flirtations, she is cased in triple brass. " Only herself" might be her motto. For anything else she does not care so much as a straw; and if the husband who is devotedly attached to her died next week, her first thought would be, How shall I look in crape and that disfiguring widow's cap ? Although she can " gush" with the utmost enthusiasm on paintings and music, and philanthropic objects, that which really interests her, and alone gives her true and profound pleasure, is the study of a new shade for her dress, or a new fashion for arranging her hair. As she dresses to perfection, she may certainly be congratulated upon have attained her end in fashionable life.

The space of time during which the men are supposed to be talking of the legislation of the nation, the foreign policy of Britain, and other sensible subjects, is a very dull and slow period to the ladies boxed up in the drawing-room.

It is impossible to get up much excitement over photograph albums filled with *cartes* of other people's friends whom you have never met, and most probably never will meet. So conversation is usually at a very low ebb until the arrival of the men. In the meantime scandal and idle gossip, with its attendant brilliant remarks, form a substitute as a sort of stop-gap. This, indeed, is not always the case, especially when really clever women are met together; but, as everybody knows, it is too generally the rule when the majority are only able to talk of persons, and not things. Liberty of speech should not be allowed to degenerate into unlimited license.

Mrs. Napier lets her eyes travel slowly and languidly over Thyrza's face and figure. An extremely plain girl, and unfortunately awkward, is her decision. No style at all about her, and her complexion quite beneath criticism.

"So you travelled with Jack," says Mrs. Napier, condescendingly.

"Only part of the way. We crossed the Channel together."

"Is he handsome?"

"Oh no."

"What is he like, Miss Rutherfurd?"

"He has grey hair," answers Thyrza, mentioning the points in Ferrier's face which have struck her most, "and blue eyes—they are grey in some lights. He has a black moustache, and he is *very* brown—browner even than I am."

"Grey hair! But he is quite a young man—scarcely thirty yet."

"He does not look old in spite of the grey hair."

"What else?"

"He had on a light grey overcoat, and a hat which looked as if the crown had been often *sat upon*. That is all I noticed, excepting that he had a lot of parcels and big boxes."

"And, Miss Rutherfurd," continues Mrs. Napier, suddenly recollecting Thyrza is Mark's protégée, and the girl proposed by him as governess for her children—"you have been at school in Villhos."

" Yes."

" Ah, I suppose you were considered the pattern girl of the school ?"

" Indeed I was not," says Thyrza, wondering why Miss Lefroy is giving her such odd little nods behind her spectacles. " I was considered the black sheep of the *pension*. The girls used to call me Beelzebub, and Beel for short, as it was rather long to say the whole name, because I was always up to some mischief."

" *My dear !*" exclaims Miss Lefroy ; " what sort of girls could they have been ?"

" Some of them were awfully jolly, but others were such sneaks, and told Miss Holt whenever we went over to the confectioner's for macaroons or bonbons. We used to slip out through the garden by a little side gate to the shop, which was next door but one to M. Paul's, and on the same side as the Flying Dragon."

" Were you found out ?" asks Mrs. Napier.

" Well, once Miss Holt came into the shop while I was buying chocolate creams for a friend of mine. I had just time to dive under the counter and crawl to the other side on my hands and knees, where I lay in fear and trembling until she had gone. One of the girls told— mean thing ! and I got no dinner for two days. But that was a *long* time ago," pursues Thyrza,

" I was only fourteen then, and quite a little girl. I have been junior English teacher for a year."

" It must have been a fine sort of teaching," says Mrs. Napier, in her soft cooing voice.

" So it was ; I got on capitally. Sometimes we acted charades, and I always took the man's part. The last time Miss Holt was scandalized because one of the girls brought a suit of her brother's old sailor's clothes to school with her, and I put them on. I made such a good man ; the girls thought I looked much nicer with a moustache than without it, and I think so too. Miss Holt was so angry, for I put my hands in my trousers pockets, and strutted and swaggered, just as I have seen petit-crevés do in Villios."

" Come here, Miss Rutherfurd," beckons Miss Lefroy, as Luke Mark and the other men enter the drawing-room. " My dear," she goes on, in a low whisper—" my dear, do not say any more about moustaches and—and—Beelzebub !"

" Ought I not to have said that ?" inquires Thyrza, horror-stricken and in the utmost consternation. " I did not know.. What shall I do ? Shall I say I did not know ?"

" No, no ; that would only make it worse."

" Do you take any interest in old china ?" asks Mr. Lefroy, briskly, rolling along the velvet-pile carpet.

"Well, yes; it is a fact I do, Mr. Lefroy," says Thyrza.

"Then you will appreciate the specimens I have gathered together. The Dresden ware I keep in this cabinet, which is all made of glass, shelves and sides, and mirrors at the back and below to reflect the figures. You will observe it has a very fine effect, and it is my own design, and you must know that *my* taste a *leetle* approaches perfection."

Mr. Lefroy pauses to regard himself with infinite satisfaction in one of the gilt girandoles above the cabinet.

"This plate, with the raised figures, is a piece of the celebrated Palissy ware. I can assure you it is rare, very rare, particularly rare. The dark-blue dish, with the gold enamel, is a specimen of Limoges, still rarer. Now, the lace on this shepherdess's dress is beautifully done, and the roses in her hair are painted by hand. Dear me! I was at considerable trouble and expense in bringing all these treasures safely to Lillieshill. It requires a very fine eye, I can tell you, to distinguish between the real and imitation Dresden."

"If you are not too tired, Miss Rutherfurd, will you give us a little music?" asks Mark. "Do you remember anything without the notes?"

Then Mr. Lefroy sits down on an ottoman near the conservatory while Thyrza goes to the piano, and he reflects that everything has gone off capitally; the fish was done to a T and cut firm and clean; there was a little too much pepper in the soup, perhaps, but otherwise it was excellent. The omelettes were tough as shoe-leather, that came of the dinner being later than usual. He must mind that another time. There is a chance for Luke now, the MacNab girls will each have 20,000*l.* down when they marry. He will promise not to spoil sport. Why, he could have either of them to-morrow for the *mere* asking, they are so awfully in love with him. That new port is really very inferior. He will send for the wine merchant's account and shut him up at once. Scarcely a drop of decent stuff to be had since Gladstone advocated cheap sherry. Showy-looking girls the MacNabs, but Mrs. Napier carries off the palm undeniably—can't hold a candle to her.

Mrs. Napier is playing Bézique with Archie MacNab, and Lola and Mark are their opponents. Without the least apparent effort, she has attracted the attention of the minister and Mr. MacNab to assist her in choosing what cards to throw away, and appeals to Mark to be told how much four kings count. " Bézique is such a frightfully intricate game, and she is so unfortunately stupid about recollecting numbers, she never can remember how much four kings count." She puts her pretty elbows, round and smooth, from which the lace sleeves have slipped back, on to the mother-o'-pearl inlaid three-legged table, and glances up into Mr. Dods' face with an innocent abandon, which makes Lola marvel how it is Mrs. Napier always contrives to look so charming, and how is it her skirts hang like those in the fashion plates, and her attitudes resemble those in a picture. In all this there is art, but it is the perfection of art and acting, for everything Charity says and does is with calculation as to the *effect* it will produce on others, and although all is studied it appears simplicity and nature itself.

Thyrza is at home at the piano; she is a born musician, and Mr. Spindler has done his best to cultivate her talent. Her fingers ramble over the keys into Ascher's San-Souci, and from that to a classical piece, a favourite of the old music master's, but thrown away upon the present audience. That style of music almost requires a special education to be appreciated, as game eaten high is not relished by the multitude. As she plays loud the conversation grows *forte;* when she plays piano, the voices sink to pianissimo.   Music always exercises a peculiarly soothing effect on Thyrza.   When angry, or vexed, or in a fit of the blues, she invariably derives consolation from her piano.   It is as good as a pipe of extra excellent tobacco to an inveterate smoker who has not smoked for twenty-four hours.

She has colours in her mind's eye for the music of different composers.   The Sonata Passione with its broad glorious chords she calls deep crimson ; Beethoven in general is rich purple with dark Rembrandt shadows thrown across the brightness of melody.   Certain compositions of Schumann recall a sunset on a clear frosty night.   Some of the old Masters twilight on a November evening, when the sun has gone behind the hills, and only a crimson glow remains in the sky with a single star shining out in the West.   The wild despairing pathos of Schumann's Manfred brings before her a picture of waves breaking on a lonely shore, with a dismasted ship floating helplessly along at the mercy of the elements.   A white rag of what has been a sail is still wrapped round the broken stump of the main-mast ; an immense wave, like a huge monster ready to devour the ill-fated vessel, is moving on towards it: there is no moon, only dull dark banks of heaving clouds.

Perhaps it is not astonishing that in her more dreamy moments, Thyrza's head is filled with odd fancies which come and go at will. Circumstances in early life mould the character to a great extent. In childhood we cannot fight against them, as we can do when older. Part of Thyrza's life has been very solitary. During the Midsummer and Christmas holidays she has always been left alone at the *pension* under the charge of an old woman called Mère Pantouffle, who with the assistance of another elderly individual cleaned the house during the absence of Miss Holt.

So she had plenty of time for dreaming, sitting in the old tree among its apple blossoms near the slow-flowing river, playing solemn mass music in the sitting room in the firelight, with Mr. Spindler accompanying her on his violin. Sauntering solitary through the chilly cloisters of the ancient convent where the nuns had paced up and down—did any thoughts of the world left outside, flit across their holy meditations?—looking out upon the gay fête-keepers at Christmas when each little peasant had his snug home to go to, while she was left to celebrate the festival with

Mère Pantouffle; always longing to take her share in the drama of life, and always obliged to stand back a spectator, she has lived more in dreamland than in reality.

As she finishes the classical piece, Mrs. Napier's low replies to Mark, and her rippling laughter at his disappointment on losing his game, warn Thyrza she is at Lillieshill.

"That's a sweet little thing," says the minister, "but I prefer something with more *tune* in it."

"Very nice, very nice," comments Mr. Lefroy, struggling violently with a strong tendency to indulge in his usual after-dinner nap. "I will show you how to play it. In books, music, pictures, it is the *style* of a thing which is everything. Even an ugly woman, if she has but style, will make a great impression, when a pretty country bumpkin would never be looked at."

"Well, it's a fact," responds Thyrza, demurely, her dark eyes flashing brilliantly, a contrast to the gravity of her countenance.

"Do you know any Scotch airs?" asks Mr. MacNab. "There's more real melody and poetry in the 'Flowers o' the Forest,' or the 'Land o' the Leal,' than in the finest operatic song."

"A very heretical opinion," answers Miss Lefroy, laughing; "the German school of music of which Miss Rutherfurd has just been giving us a specimen is all the fashion now."

"I cannot be troubled with the German school," rejoins Mr. MacNab; "I like the old-fashioned tunes best, although I daresay it is not the *thing*."

Thyrza begins a selection of Scotch reels arranged by Mr. Spindler, which she gives with such spirit that Mr. MacNab rocks up and down, keeping time with his feet; in fact, he would snap his fingers, were not his wife casting wrathful glances of indignation at him. Mrs. MacNab is not proud of the low descent of her husband, and would fain send to the *Heralds'* office for a crest and coat of arms, but MacNab, while not caring one whit who knows of his parentage, and having the good sense not to flourish it in every one's face, will not allow his wife to do anything of the kind. So she has, perforce, to content herself with having monograms painted in divers shapes and forms all over Quentinshope.

"Bravo! bravo! Miss Rutherfurd," cries Mr. MacNab, rising to wish Miss Lefroy good evening, the carriages having been brought round; "I have not heard the like of that playing these twenty years. Will you be in this neighbourhood in the autumn?"

"I do not know," returns Thyrza, smiling.

"Because if you are, you must come to our ball in October. It is to be given for Lola's coming of age."

"Thanks, I am not sure, but if I am it will delight me extremely."

"Miss Lefroy says you have some relations in Scotland,—Mr. Rutherfurd, of High Riggs. You'll be certain to stay with your grandfather?"

This is an awkward question, for old Mr. Rutherfurd has announced in plain terms he will have nothing to do with Thyrza.

"I think not," she answers.

"Ah, well, but if possible you must come. Archie there, is splendid at the Highland Fling."

"Is that a Scotch song ?—is it pretty ?" inquires Thyrza.

"No," says Mr. MacNab, with a hearty laugh, "it's a Scotch dance. The autumn is a long while off yet, but if you are in Scotland you must dance the reel of Hoolachin with me. If you are not at Lillieshill, you will come and pay us a visit at Quentins, I hope, whenever we settle to have the ball. So it's *a promise*."

CHAPTER V.

"DOES the sun annoy you, Miss Thyrza?" asks Luke Mark.

" No, not at all. I like to feel it shining on my face."

" Ah, you see you have no wrinkles or crows feet to be revealed. What is it like to be sweet seventeen, and all one's life before you?"

" Very pleasant indeed, Mr. Mark. Seventeen! Why, I shall live thirty years, at any rate, yet. Fancy thirty whole years, in which *some* nice things *must* happen."

" Would you mind moving a little more to the left?" he pursues, standing in a reflective attitude before his picture, his head thrown slightly back with a critical air, a pipe in his mouth, and his hands in his trousers pockets. He has established his easel and painting apparatus under the spreading branches of a fine old beech tree on the lawn near the house.

It is a lovely June morning. The sun shines on the glittering dew still quivering like so many precious stones in the white and yellow ox-eyed daisies; the blue, misty mountain peaks cutting the clear air asunder, and the beech leaves in the Lillieshill woods murmur to each other that this is the blessed summer time; that next year they will lie dead, faded, sodden, and rotten underfoot; so they will drink their fill of the sun while it shines, of the sweets of lilies and the bloom of roses, will laugh to the moon and glisten white in its beams; for say they, with the Pagans of old, " Let us eat, let us drink, for to-morrow we die."

How sweet the air is, loaded with the perfume of lilacs and hawthorn flowers. The day is still young; the sun's rays have not their full noonday strength yet, and can hardly penetrate through the dense overhanging leaves and branches in which a breeze creates a thousand simultaneous dissolving lights and shadows.

On the mossy banks by the pond and the cascade the grasshoppers are clicking away among the speedwells and my lady's bedstraw, and little grey rabbits, with white scuds, rustle abruptly out of sight into the copsewood from a field of growing corn, in which, if the farmer discovered them, they know some leaden pellets would soon end their career.

"I thought so; the light *is* wrong. It should fall a little more on the left cheek, consequently, on this shoulder. I see now. A few more touches will just do it," removing one hand from his trousers-pocket. He then takes up his mahl-stick, and raising it to a level with his eyes, shuts one, and, to the uninitiated observer, squints ferociously.

The picture is a portrait of Thyrza, representing her in a red gipsy-cloak, holding a basket of flowers in her hand. Behind are trees and an ancient stone balustrade, through the bars of which shine the waters of a brook. The stag-like eyes, with a pensive dreamy look in them, are almost too wild for beauty; they seem to require taming; but they give one an idea of possessing a wonderful power of expression and feeling in their hazel depths. The complexion is olive, the mouth rather pouting, the nose delicate and not very determined in shape, the brow low and wide, from which the dark brown hair grows back in rippling undulations and rich heavy masses. Originally Mark had sketched in a flower-girl, dressed in white and rose coloured satin, with a necklace of pearls and a white embroidered handkerchief tied loosely under her chin. However, finding the fit of the body troublesome, he gave it up, and retaining the former attitude, painted out the bodice, drawing in Thyrza's face and cloak instead.

"We've an hour to ourselves," continues Mark. "Uncle Richard is safe until breakfast."

"What is he doing?"

"Exercising the turtle, and after that he is going to blow up the under-gardener; I don't know what about. I am afraid I shall be obliged to rub out the face with turpentine. The eyes don't do at all. They are too far apart by the eighth of an inch."

"Oh, I hope not," says Thyrza.

In her secret soul she is not partial to "sitting," and regards the picture as interminable, Mark having a habit of painting right out one day the labour of weeks.

"Oh, they are quite wrong. However, I can easily alter them."

"When do you think it will be finished?"

"Oh, some time or other," he replies, indefinitely. "I shall come to Carmylie and get a sitting there occasionally, and by-and-by, I dare say, Mrs. Napier will allow you to come over to Lillieshill from Saturday until Monday. This is only the first painting. I wish I had the eyes right. After all, I don't believe there is much wrong with them. Be a bore to alter them, and then find they had been right at first. Don't look quite so serious; it gives a disagreeable expression to the corners of the mouth. Try to smile."

Thyrza breaks into a merry laugh. Mark is the least thing in the world provoked.

"Oh, Mr. Mark, I shall be grave directly; but I do so want to laugh when I see you looking so solemnly at me and measuring, just as if I was somebody not real, you know. It is so ridiculous."

"Try again," says Mark, good-humouredly. "I am not quite certain about the proportions. I want to measure your face, and you may laugh as much as you like while I do that."

He takes a letter from his pocket and measures the length of Thyrza's face. It divides exactly into three parts from the forehead to the chin. Near the porch on the sweep is a figure of a fat man in light summer attire. Mr. Lefroy is waddling along to Mark with the utmost haste. Being very stout and rotund, it occupies him several minutes to traverse the distance of fifty yards.

"Now keep grave this time," pursues Mark.

A lively wasp flies near Thyrza, coming unpleasantly close to her face. She stands patiently, not venturing to move, and appeals to Mark.   He gets up from his camp-stool, pursues the wasp enthusiastically with his pocket-handkerchief, and seats himself, when it returns, buzzing irritatingly in close proximity with his aquiline nose, on which it manifests a decided intention to crawl.

"Bother that brute!" he exclaims, having again routed the enemy and once more settled himself with his palette on his thumb and picked up the right brush for painting skin and not that for laying on masses of colour. "*Con*found it! That's the nuisance of summer!   One can't sit outside for a minute without being surrounded by a flying host.   What's become of the smoothing brush and the little palette knife?   I believe I've upset the megilp.   No I haven't.   I am going to sketch in the arm, so will you put down that piece of paper and hold the basket for the attitude of the elbow?   Don't move for the life of you.   I will see about the paper."

"And do tell me whose likeness is on the paper, Mr. Mark.   I've wanted to know ever since I came here.   I found it in my box the night of my arrival."

Suiting the action to the word, he moves away the drawing.   It has hitherto been turned with the blank side upwards; now it is reversed, and the woman's face Thyrza had admired looks up at him.

"Good God!" he cries, recoiling back several steps and becoming ashy white. "My wife!"

"What is the matter, Mr. Mark?" exclaims Thyrza, oblivious of the position that has taken so much time in arranging, and letting the basket fall to the ground. "Oh, don't tear it up. Are you really a married man? You don't look in the least as if you were."

"Why? Are there particular signs which denote a married man?" says he.

"Oh, I thought people looked much graver and older when they were married."

"Now, Miss Thyrza, no one knows I have a wife excepting that lady herself, her unlucky husband, and the man who read the service for us."

"Not even Mr. Ferrier?"

"No, I should think Jack did not know," he answers almost fiercely.

"But I thought he was your greatest friend," stammers Thyrza.

"So he is. But it is not convenient to let even your best friend into the whole of your secrets. However, you must not laugh when you hear aunt or uncle talking of my future marriage, and so on."

"No"—hesitatingly.

"In short, I wish you to keep the knowledge of my wife a secret. It cannot touch or hurt you in any way, or I would not ask it. All you have to do is simply to say nothing."

Mr. Lefroy bearing down upon them within a couple of yards prevents Thyrza from being able to do more than give a hasty answer in the affirmative.

"Oh, Luke, I can hardly speak of it," says Mr. Lefroy, mournfully—"that idiot of a Jenkins!"

"Has Europa sprained her leg, or is Jupiter off his feet?"

"The turtle which was getting on so nicely! I had the poor dear thing out to exercise a little by the pond, and left Jenkins in charge while I went up to the gardens to see how the tomatoes are getting on, and when I came back it was gone. *Actually gone!* I shall have the pond dragged, but I shall never see it again. And to think what fine soup it would have made! I really think, Luke," continues Mr. Lefroy, plaintively, "I really think the severe loss will have a great effect on my health for some-time."

"You should have the pond dragged."

"I shall; but the turtle is lost for ever. The

largest one I ever saw alive in this country.
Ah! how is the portrait progressing? Let me
put a few touches in that corner to show you
the sort of thing it wants."

" Oh! don't trouble," rejoins Mark, hastily.
" I know what you mean."

" You can't until I have shown you," pursues
Mr. Lefroy. Every one considers himself at
liberty to criticise the production of an amateur.
Even a person who can scarcely distinguish an
oil painting from a water colour will have no
scruple in pronouncing judgment upon the unfortunate amateur. " There is something queer
about the eyes. Don't you think there is a
slight *cast* in one?"

Mr. Lefroy seizes hold of the palette and
mixes some colours, preparing to execute his
improvements, when the gong sounds for breakfast.

" What is the thermometer to-day?" Mark
asks adroitly, as they draw near the house.

" Bless me! bless me! I had forgotten to
look. What a lucky thing you reminded me,"
and he trots off to the tree in which the thermometer is fastened.

" Then I can *rely* upon you?" says Mark to
Thyrza, while entering the dining-room where
Miss Lefroy is waiting, and she replies quickly—

"Yes, you can."

A breakfast table in a Scotch country house is one of the pleasantest sights possible belonging to the material senses. How picturesque to the hungry eye is the dish of trout, fried in butter and oatmeal; the snowy scones laid in damask napkins; the golden marmalade and heather-honey; the crisp oatcakes; the abundant choice of various sweets; and later on, the cold grouse or capercailzie; while added to all this the steamy scent of coffee or chocolate breathes an agreeable invitation to begin!

The sun streams brightly through the French windows and half closed persiennes on to the white cloth, silver hissing tea-urn, and a " bit " of rich colouring by Meissonier on the wall. Miss Lefroy's peacocks, impatient for their break-fast, come and tap on the panes to remind her time is on the wing, and that they are on the look out for their breadcrumbs. At Lillieshill, the custom is to open the post-bag before breakfast, and arrange the letters for each person in a little heap at the side of his plate. Whether this be a good plan or not, it is the regular system.

Some visitors, stronger minded than others, exercised sufficient self-control, after turning over their epistle to ascertain the post-mark—

an instinct common with every one—to place the document in their pockets, thus enabling them to eat their breakfasts with a good digestion and quiet pulse.

There is a large pile awaiting Mark, on which Miss Lefroy comments playfully.

" What a pretty monogram there is on one of your letters, Luke. You have got quite a general post-office to-day."

" Do you want the monogram for some of the girls who are collecting crests ?" he returns, opening a letter nonchalantly and tearing off the purple and silver monogram for Miss Lefroy.

" Thanks. What is the name ? Luke, Louisa ; no, it is none of those. One can never make head or tail of these unintelligible twists and curves. This might be Greek or Hebrew, or Chinese, for any word that can be deciphered."

" Lilith," answers Mark, placidly. " She is a friend of mine in London, and wants me to get her one of those Skye terriers without beginning or end. I am to telegraph immediately from Queensmuir as to when I think I can obtain it. Mrs. Temple will probably kill it with kindness for a month, and then it will be discarded for some newer attraction."

"What was the height of the thermometer, Richard?"

"Sixty-five in the shade. The cook is getting very careless about the cutlets, and the coffee is not fit to drink."

"You had better speak to her."

"I shall when I order the dinner."

Mr. Lefroy is very emphatic on the subject, and to hear him speak one would think him the greatest autocrat that ever lived, whereas the mistress of the kitchen who ministers to his epicurean tastes rules him with a rod of iron, and is in reality the head of the house.

"I am thinking of going to Queensmuir immediately," says Mark, rising from the table. "If any one has any commands I shall be happy to fulfil them."

"My box of after-dinner pills is finished, Luke. You can tell the chemist to make up another dozen. Should recommend you to try them. Composition of my own. The chemist said he had never seen anything like the prescription."

"Then I am off," rejoins Mark. "Have not you got any shades of wool that want matching for that voluminous sofa blanket you are working for a Sandwich Island chief, Aunt Fanny?"

" Don't be irreverent, Luke. It's going to be sold for the S. P. G. But even if I did want any worsted you would never match the mauves."

" Don't forget the pills, Luke," calls out Mr. Lefroy, as Mark leaves the room on his way to the stables.

" What would you like to do to-day, Thyrza ?" Miss Lefroy has arrived at the familiarity of Thyrza's Christian name. " Have a ride, dear ? I must call on Lord and Lady George Boggs. That would be no amusement to you, they are both so deaf, and talking for an hour through an ear-trumpet is very exhausting. Do you know ' Tupper's Proverbial Philosophy ?' "

" No," says Thyrza.

" There is such capital advice in it about matrimony. It advises all girls to pray for a good husband, and whether they get him or not it can do the man no harm and most likely will benefit him. A good husband is the best present a girl can have ; it is better than money, better than good looks, better than cleverness. There is a mate born for every one."

" Then what became of yours ?" asks Thyrza. " Oh, I beg——"

" He must have died in the cradle, for he did not come up to time, you see," returns Miss

Lefroy, not in the least offended. " However, I hope yours has not shared the same misfortune. It is a dreary life to be a governess, always among little children."

" Horrid pests," says Thyrza.

" Oh, I like children ; but it must be tiresome teaching them, unless you have a born love of teaching implanted in you. You are a nice little girl, I have taken a fancy to you, and I hope you will spend your holidays at Lillieshill. But I think you are right in going to work at Carmylie ; it is preferable to being dependent on your relations, and Luke is still rather young to have a ward of your age. Well, dear, go and put on your habit and be back in time for lunch, if you can."

Then Mr. Lefroy says grace and departs to the kitchen to deliver his opinions on the subject of the cutlets to the housekeeper, and consult with her concerning the great event of the day —dinner; and Miss Lefroy, wearing an enormous slop-basin hat, which swallows up her small thin face, comes out of the conservatory with a plate of breadcrumbs for the pet peacocks. She watches Thyrza, in an old dark blue habit, formerly Miss Lefroy's, canter down the avenue, and then, feeling a little sad with the thought of the vanished time when she herself was young and lighthearted as the girl rider, she turns to caress the peacocks standing round her picking up the crumbs, after which she goes to clip the dead leaves and withered flowers from her plants. She takes no part in the housekeeping, Mr. Lefroy transacts everything connected with it himself, thereby sparing his sister a great amount of work and annoyance.

No go-between—on the important matter of eating—would content Mr. Lefroy. This settled, Mr. Lefroy walks round his Home Farm, talks to his grieve (farm bailiff), looks at the turnips; thinks the editor of the *Kilniddryshire Advertiser* is a smart pushing fellow, quite took *his* view of that case. Shall ask him to Lillieshill for a couple of days' partridge shooting in the autumn; comes home to lunch; drives into the country; criticises his flowers and grapes; has afternoon tea; writes letters; dinner; has a nap, snores; protests " Fanny *always* thinks he is asleep, if he closes his eyes for two seconds, when on the contrary he was just thinking of a patent swivel;" has coffee, reads *The Field* and *The Times*, and is sure he knows better than " that correspondent," and goes to bed convinced there are not many more enlightened men in the world than himself.

Luke Mark drives into Queensmuir, and puts up

at the Carmylie Arms inn. The Queensmuirians stare at him in wonder and great admiration, as though they had never beheld a human being before.

Queensmuir is a little manufacturing town, not unlike Villios in its narrow, ill paved, and worst lighted winding streets, with odd unexpected corners, and "wynds" or "closes," up which the wind blows when apparently there is none anywhere else.

It is irregularly built; some of the houses being several stories high, and others short and low, as if they had received a knock on the head, preventing their further growth.

Hills, blue as the Franconian range of which the Transatlantic poet sings so sweetly, surround Queensmuir on all sides.

Excepting from the west end it is impossible to enter the town, unless by ascending or descending rising ground.

In winter and when the roads are bad, which happens whenever there is a rainy day, the weather acting the parts of road maker and scavenger, this last mentioned feature in the landscape is a consideration.

Things never having been different in Queensmuir, no one remonstrates.

The discontent with the state of existing circumstances evaporates in a hearty fit of grumbling, when the time comes for paying the road assessments.

Besides, nothing can be done in Queensmuir without the consent of the Baron Bailie, whose ideas on all subjects by no means tally with those of the Queensmuirians. They may fret and fume as they like, explode in wrath in letters to the *Kilniddryshire Advertiser*, to ventilate their troubles according to the general custom when any one has a grievance, but the Bailie holds his own, and administers his authority after his own lights, in defiance of the combined strength of the whole Parochial Board.

A great deal of business is transacted in Queensmuir, it being the terminus town for a pretty extensive distinct of glen and hill country.

Of competition there is none; two butchers rule the roast, and determine the price of beef for a population of upwards of 4000 inhabitants. There is only one house-painter, and other trades are represented in proportion. The shopkeepers, having their regular customers, and knowing the next town, Middleby, to be at an inconvenient distance for those persons living in the country, are thoroughly independent. They *will* receive your money if you choose to patronize them with your custom, but if you like to transfer it elsewhere, you are at perfect

liberty to do so, and they will not exert themselves in any way to retain it.

Society, properly so called, does not exist,
Queensmuir being split up into numerous petty
factions, owing to internal disputes, and only
two families on an average in the place, are on
speaking terms with the whole community.

Marriages are, on the whole, numerous among
the lower classes; the new year and the terms
Whitsuntide and Martinmas being the favourite
times of the year, but there is a deadlock among
the young ladies from lack of suitors, their equals
in rank, and the majority of them stand an excellent chance of becoming old maids, unless some
wave of good fortune should bring into Queensmuir
a small army of clerks, ministers, and others with
salaries varying from two to three hundred a year,
and each, like Cœlebs, in search of a wife.

Such an advent would be hailed with pleasure
by the fathers and brothers, who do not admire
the foreboding that their daughters and sisters
will probably remain on their hands altogether,
for, whatever may be said to the contrary, the
men of the family are never averse to see their
unattached feminine belongings enter into the
longed for Canaan of matrimony.

In Queensmuir there are ten kirks, not counting the Episcopal Church, and also four banks,

from which it may be inferred that the souls and purses alike of the lieges of the burgh are well taken care of.

A Town House, lately renovated and beautified, adorns the High Street, and a large gilt salamander or dragon looks down from the parish kirk steeple over the worthy burghers. S. Bridget is the patron saint.

It probably is not the correct thing for *all* towns to have patron saints. Be this as it may, Queensmuir boasts one—a relic, no doubt, of the " Pope, that Pagan full of pride," the mere mention of whom is sufficient to make many Queensmuirians feel as uncomfortable as though the " Great Sooty Original," horns and all, were visible among them. But S. Bridget is not so much reverenced as the stronger spirit, S. Whisky; people in general seeming to prefer the tangible and concrete substance to the abstract and unseen.

Many superstitions still linger in Queensmuir. Hallowe'en is observed, old style, when the gardens of the bachelors in the vicinity of the town are pillaged by the unmarried women for *kale stocks*, Anglicè, plants of kale. They must be gathered in the dark, and are placed behind the doors of their houses, when the first man who comes in the morning will, it is supposed, be the future husband.

The crowing of a cock at untimeous hours is firmly regarded as an omen of death or misfortune, also the howling of a dog at night; and a brood of chickens which turn out all hens is considered very unlucky.

The Queensmuirians look down with patronizing contempt on the dwellers in the glens as "country bodies wha ken naething," and the country bodies think Queensmuir an amazingly large city.

Instead of going to the post-office, which is kept by an old shopkeeper of a pious turn of mind and a remarkable shortness of temper— two attributes that not unfrequently accompany each other—Mark wends his way to one of the four banks. Probably he intends despatching his telegram about the Skye terrier afterwards. This bank, called the British Jute Company, is a square, dingy, dirty-grey house, fronting the High Street and the Town House. It is the essence of neatness and respectability within and without. Woe betide the hapless spider who spins its web in Mrs. Hislop's dining or drawing-room cornice! woe to the unfortunate domestic who should venture to take an extra half hour in bed on washing morning! and woe to that individual who should mar the spotless expanse of the clean doorstep by forgetting to scrape the mud of Queensmuir off his feet!

Mr. Hislop, the banker, is considered more in the light of a friend and confidential adviser of the Lillieshill family than as a mere man of business. Besides being a banker, he is also a " writer" or lawyer, and conducts the cases under the Sheriff in the Small Debt Courts, held in the Town House every month. In appearance he is not unlike a penguin, with pale blue eyes, and is fast growing ponderous in corporation. Most of the county families bank at the B. J. C., and more than half of them employ Mr. Hislop as their factor. In consequence of this, Mr. Hislop is disposed to regard the county families as men and women very superior indeed to the class of which he himself forms a worthy member. He is asked out to dinner once or twice every year at the best houses, where he enjoys a good dinner with good wine. And at those places at which he is rather a favourite, he is generally invited over for some days' shooting in the autumn.

All this is greatly relished by his bustling, sharp-tempered, warm-hearted wife. When Mrs. Hislop has dined at Lillieshill, she usually has a party a few evenings afterwards, at which she amuses her friends and neighbours by quoting secondhand the sayings and doings of old Lord and Lady George Bogg, thus impressing the Queensmuirians with a sense of her importance and intimacy with the " upper ten" of the county. Mr. and Mrs. Hislop have two sons and a daughter—Tertius, Tom, and Robertina. The former is intended to follow in his father's footsteps, while Tom is to be a medical man. At present he is employed in his father's bank as clerk, and a nice time Mr. Jardine, the accountant, has in making him do his work, Tom being much more inclined to drawing caricatures in the bank books and play tricks, than add up columns of figures and estimate the rate of discount. The Miss MacNabs, in a pony carriage from Long Acre, and a diminutive tiger perched behind, have just driven across the High Street, attended by sundry admiring urchins, who are holding on in the background, when they pull up to speak to Mr. Dods.

"Tertius, the MacNabs are talking to Cousin James," says Tom, stopping in the middle of a declaration he is writing out for Mr. Hislop, to step down from his three-legged stool and look through the black wire blinds that have been put up to prevent the clerks from gazing out and the Queensmuirians from staring in.

"Is Mr. Hislop at home?" asks Mark, pushing back the red baize swing doors, and entering the bank.

A shock head of light brown hair, a pair of blue eyes speckled with black spots, and a very small nose, which constitute the chief traits in Tom Hislop's physiognomy, is turned round for Mark's observation from his post. Tom has expected to see Mr. Jardine, and is not disappointed to behold instead Mark's pleasant, good-looking face.

"Yes, he is."

"I want to speak to him," pursues Mark.

Mr. Hislop is sitting in his private room talking over some business matters with Mr. Jardine. He rises on hearing Mark wishes to see him, and the accountant goes out into the bank.

"All well at Lillieshill, I hope?" says Mr. Hislop. "Mr. Lefroy is thinking of sending his cattle to Battersea soon, I believe?"

"Oh yes; all well." Then Mark hesitates a little.

"The roads really pretty fair?" observes Mr. Hislop.

"Yes, I did not notice; I suppose they are."

Mark appears to find some difficulty in explaining himself. Mr. Hislop does not know how to assist him. He wishes his wife were here. Helena is always capital in an emergency of this kind.

"I want you to transact a little business for me," begins Mark. "I need hardly say I have known you so long, Mr. Hislop, that I can depend upon it being strictly between ourselves, and going no further."

Mr. Hislop peers cautiously round him, sees that the door is slightly ajar, closes it softly, and says—

"Mr. Mark, if it is within the power of mortal man I will do what I can. You may trust me."

This is with a reservation. If Mrs. Hislop has not seen Mark in Queensmuir, she will ask no inconvenient questions; but if she becomes aware of the fact, then Mr. Hislop knows she will persecute him at night until, from sheer weariness, he may be induced to answer her, and partially reveal the truth. Mr. Hislop likes his night's rest, and, if possible, wishes to serve his client also. But what can be the business? Can Mark have failed and lost his money? Or does he want to buy shares in some company, or in the cargo of a merchant vessel? Mr. Hislop not long ago realized a comfortable sum by sending out salt to a country unprovided with that condiment. Or has Mark come to inquire about a shooting, or to rent a house in the neighbourhood?

"A friend of mine who has made an unfortunate marriage, and does not wish his name to appear in the transaction, has commissioned me to act for him in this case," says Mark, a brilliant inspiration seizing him to represent himself by an imaginary friend; "I thought I could not apply to a better person than yourself. My friend has, therefore, asked me to lend him a hundred pounds in the meantime, which he will repay me through his London bankers. He intends to pay his wife two hundred pounds per quarter."

"Yes," says Mr. Hislop. "You are confident of your friend's good faith?"

He is astonished, but he gives no sign of amazement. The friend seems rather a doubtful reality. In his own experience of men, he has invariably found that it was "every one for himself, and let the weakest go to the wall." Mark's ready compliance to lend money to his friend is incomprehensible. To the hard-headed, shrewd Scotchman it is inexplicable. He judges others by himself, and is certain *he* would not have done so. But Mark has mentioned that the money is for a woman, which to Mr. Hislop's mind explains everything. People have always a motive for their actions, and probably Mark's is to oblige the lady.

"Most decidedly I have confidence in my friend."

"I presume he and his wife are separated from each other?" goes on Mr. Hislop.

"Yes, they are," rejoins Mark. "I am out of a cheque-book at present; I should like to send the first cheque by this post. On the 30th of this month will you despatch the two hundred pounds?"

"Will you favour me with the name of the party to whom the cheque is payable?"

"Lilith Dawson," writes Mark.

"I fear that is a bad pen, Mr. Mark," interrupted Mr. Hislop. "I use fine-pointed pens, but perhaps you prefer a broader point."

"I like a quill in general," says Mark, writing the address for Mr. Hislop with a quill, and blotting the paper on a new blotting-pad. "It may be as well to scrawl a few lines to my friend to let him know I have done as he wished."

"Very true, Mr. Mark." Understanding from Mark's manner that he does not care to be further interrogated on the subject of this friend who is separated from his wife. He has already decided that Mark must be acquainted with her, or else the friend must pay heavy interest for the loan. It is highly improbable a business man would lend money on any other terms. Then Mark has brought no papers about it. There ought to have been some sort of an agreement surely? However, he ought to know his own affairs best. Still, as an old friend of Mark's, he must utter one more protest.

"Mr. Mark, I trust your friend's finances are all right. Your good nature should not lead you into trouble. One of the nicest and most promising young men I ever knew was ruined by being surety for a friend."

"Have I not told you, Mr. Hislop, that I shall get it back again?" answers Mark, folding up the letter he has written to his wife, and placing the cheque inside the paper in the envelope, directed with the broad quill charged very full with ink. "I have written the cheque for June 30th—I mean, filled in the name of the lady for you."

"Although your friend's name is not to appear, have you any objection to yours? When I send the money, shall I say, 'To Lilith Dawson, from Luke Mark?'"

"It will not signify about my name. She

will suppose I have something to do with the lawyer," he replies, drying the envelope on the blotting-pad.

Mr. Hislop often takes his county visitors upstairs to have a glass of wine and a biscuit; but he does not ask Mark to-day. He knows all the skeletons and secret histories of nearly every family in Kilniddryshire, and he wishes he could see the lady to whom such a liberal allowance is made. He would lay a heavy odds that she is handsome. While he is in the short passage leading from the Bank front door to the stairs, the accountant, having left his pencil in Mr. Hislop's private room, returns for it. The blotting-pad is lying wide open, and the direction has been clearly impressed. With a very little trouble, Mr. Jardine manages to decipher it. He does not remain much longer than to look at the direction and pick up his pencil.

When Mr. Hislop is once more seated in his room, he draws his table towards him and glances over the writing-case. Like the accountant, his eye is attracted by the black direction on the white blotting-pad—

"MADAME DAWSON,

"—— Place,

"Bayswater,

"London, W.,"

he reads. " He said he wrote to his *friend*," he exclaims, settling his thumbs in his waistcoat. " He wrote to the *woman*. The friend does not exist. I knew he did not from the begin-ning."

CHAPTER VI.

THE day has fulfilled the most sanguine expectations of its fineness, which is more than can be said for the generality of earthly anticipations. It is nearly two o'clock, the hour at which Mr. Lefroy lunches and waits for neither man nor woman, be he or she prince or princess. The soup or the entrées might spoil if not served at the exact moment, and to a gourmand like Mr. Lefroy, this misfortune would certainly trouble his dreams or render his pillow a sleepless one.

About a mile and a half from Lillieshill is an old bridge called the Bridge of Bogg. It is an ancient structure, very narrow, and only admitting of one carriage or cart crossing at the same time. It is built of greystone, and consists of a single pointed arch, having a kelpie's* head graven on each side above the date of erection, and the coronet and coat-of-arms of the baron at whose expense it was there placed.

---

* A kelpie is a water sprite.

Near the bridge is a mill, broad-eaved, thatched roof, and grey with age. Over it some pigeons, with coral feet and glossy breasts, are flying, while others sit on the chimney-top, pluming themselves. The burn, after turning the great black lichen-grown wheel, tumbles precipitously down to the Bogg, the sunbeams glinting into prismatic colours as the water leaps from one wide spoke to another.

In the doorway stands the miller enveloped in a cloud of dust, wherein the light makes golden ladders: woodbine climbs, trained on lines of string, round the casement window; a row of gorgeous dwarf sunflowers grow in front, stacks of peat and unhewn pine logs are piled against the wall, close to which a cart is propped up. From the shafts a man, who is talking to the miller, has just unloosened a black Flanders horse; its mane and tail are carefully plaited and ornamented with gay ribbons. On the threshold a large collie dog, tawny of muzzle and sleek of coat, sleeps in an attitude of perfect ease and repose; hens with variegated feathers and scarlet combs cluck to downy chickens, scratching among the little flower-beds, to the serious injury of the double red daisies and pansies: the song of a canary from its cage comes loudly through the unclosed door.

On the brae-side the broom is out in a glory of living splendour, extending far up the steep, sandy scour, where pink spikes of foxglove blow and rabbits have their warrens, and martens bore nests, making even the hanging grape-like blossoms of the laburnums pale and faint before the dazzling magnificence of the golden ocean. Tall ash trees, their plumy leaves fresh from the black buds, rear their branches towards heaven wreathed with a tangled network of graceful ivy, silver-barked beeches, gnarled wych elms, and rowans crowned with " blossom-balls" of foam meet in wild confusion above; while down by the clear amber waters of the Bogg, flowing over the russet sandstone rocks, grow bushes of red-and-white dog-roses, clumps of meadow-sweet, cuckoo flowers, and yellow arum lilies.

In a meadow hard by, cattle graze up to their fetlocks in luxuriant pasturage, sprinkled with fragrant clover and starred with daisies and buttercups. Brown ridges of moorland, which a few months further on will be flushed with purple heather, flanked by belts of woodland and strips of cornfields, and an occasional cottage or farmstead, rise in undulations above the brae.

Seated on the parapet of the bridge is Thyrza. Her hat is on her lap, and she is fastening some sprays of golden broom in the front of it.   Her pony feeds on a juicy bit of grass sticking out from the stones in the bridge, and its reins are thrown over her right arm. She finishes her task, and picking up stone after stone, throws them down into the water, watching the splash they make, and amused by the flop caused by their striking the water.

A man in a suit of light tweed and a white hat, with a large puggeree placed well on the back of his head, comes slowly down the brae. Behind him is a small shaggy dog, long bodied, short legged, a mass of hair like an animated muff. Thyrza, roused from her reverie by the sound of Ferrier's tread on the dusty road, turns round.

"Well, mademoiselle, how has the world been using you since I last saw you?" he asks, sitting down beside her on the mossy rain-worn parapet.

"Oh, very kindly, monsieur," she replies.

"Does Mark let you ride about the country without an escort?"

"No, the groom was with me, but coming home his horse cast a shoe, and he stayed behind at the blacksmith's to have it put on."

"And what do you do with yourself all day?"

"Nothing but sleep, eat, drink, and so on. Mr. Mark is painting a picture of me, and I usually sit for it every morning."

"You have got on pretty well, considering you have only been a month at Lillieshill. Is Mark at home?"

"He was not when I set off for my ride, but I should think he will be on my return."

"And you like Lillieshill better than the *pension?*"

"Oh, there is no comparison."

"But you must have had friends there! Girls are gregarious; they always form gushing attachments and write long letters in a thin, angular hand, all crossed and delightfully illegible."

"Yes, I had some school friends; but I don't suppose I shall see any of them again. My greatest friends were Mr. Spindler, M. Paul the barber, and two dear old toads that lived in the garden. They buried themselves every winter, and came up again in the spring."

"Interesting objects for pets! And *who* was M. Paul?"

"He has a shop next door but one to the confectioner's, close to the Flying Dragon. Such a nice old man! He was very kind to me."

"You seem to have had a choice selection of acquaintances in Villios?"

" Oh, Miss Holt knew lots of people, but she was different from *me*.   M. Paul took me to the theatre."

" Tall, thin man ?   He cut my hair the day I left Villios."

" Yes, tall and thin with no hair on his head— not even *one* hair.   He used to make cosmetics for producing a ' luxuriant crop;' but they never did *him* any good.   Did you ever hear of Egmont ?"

" No; who was he ?   Was he a relation of the barber's ?"

" A Flemish Count, who was beheaded by the Duke of Alba, in 1568.   The play that M. Paul took me to see was about him."

" And when did you and the barber go to the theatre ?"

" Last Christmas.   Miss Holt went to pay a visit to some friends in Paris, and I was left alone in the *pension*."

" In that great dull house ?"

" Yes.   There was an old woman, Mère Pantouffle, who cooked my dinner and slept in the house at night.   Oh, monsieur, I did feel so desolate, and I sat looking out of the music-room window——"

" Out of which you jumped so nicely."

" On to the street," continues Thyrza, heedless

of his interruption, "which was filled with people all in fête dresses. And I was cross with everything. It was so dismal—so dead—so stupid—so stagnant. Just as I was complaining to myself, Mère Pantouffle said some one wanted to speak to me. It was M. Paul."

"But how came you to be on such friendly terms with him?"

"Why, monsieur, he coiffed Miss Holt's hair. She used to send me across to his shop with her chignons for him to rearrange when the fashion changed. No one minded. M. Paul said he was going to the theatre, and if I liked he would take me with him. He saw I was dying of *ennui* by myself, and I had known him ever since I lived at Villios. So in the evening he came for me."

"Was he a married man?"

"Oh yes; Madame Paul was a fat *little* woman, like a roly-poly pudding, with a string tied round the middle to indicate her waist."

"Had they any sons?"

"Yes, two. · Louis and Victor."

"Were they of the party too?"

"No, they could not come. Louis is in a coiffeur's shop in Paris, and Victor is a commis-voyageur for M. Joachim. What questions you ask, monsieur!"

"I merely thought it probable the sons were there also."

"They were very polite young men, and sometimes paid me some pretty compliments."

"Oh, you like the polite way of telling lies?"

"Yes—at least, I mean I like people who say nice things."

"Whether they are true or not?"

"Oh, they may occasionally be true, may they not?"

"When you have lived a little longer, you will find it is not your best friends who pay you the most compliments."

"Well, perhaps not. But a word of praise, how it helps one on, and makes one so bright and gay! Perhaps I should tire of compliments if I were more accustomed to them. One does weary of things after awhile," looking meditative and tapping her boot with her silver-mounted riding-whip.

"I should just think one did!" says Ferrier. "You see," very gravely, "there is nothing new under the sun. And it is even very stale and hackneyed to say there is nothing new. All the inventions, as they are called, have already been in existence since the beginning of the world, they are only put into a different shape and form. The description of the fast man is as applicable now as it was in Solomon's day. The only difference is, there was no smoking then. But if they had known the virtue of the weed, how they would have smoked! for of course there was a tobacco plant among the other plants and shrubs in the Garden of Eden. But you were telling me about the Villios barber."

" Whom you seem to despise."

" No, in general I don't care for the snob-ocracy; but very likely he was an intelligent man. He must have been if he took you to the theatre. Did you enjoy it?"

" Oh, ciel! how beautiful it was!" cried Thyrza, enthusiastically. "All the lights, and colours, and finely dressed people, and the music."

" What is the story of Egmont?" asks Ferrier, lighting a cigar.

" The first scene is nothing particular. There are soldiers and citizens talking about the Regent and Egmont. Oh, what I liked best was the lovely piece where Egmont comes with his court dress, covered over by a military cloak, to see Clärchen. She was his ' geliebte.' "

" His what?"

" His sweetheart—his true love, you know,

monsieur," explains Thyrza. "She is standing
in her humble cottage, just in her peasant's
dress, and her hair braided down her back in two
long pigtails tied with blue ribbons. She is
only a peasant, one of the people; but Egmont
is so noble, and feels for them. Clärchen wor-
ships him; and I am not astonished, for he is so
grand—like a god. The cottage is dark at first,
then the light is turned on fuller, and as
Egmont takes off his cloak and stands before
Clärchen in all the splendour of his courtier's
dress and his manhood's prime, one feels he is
worth loving, not only for his beauty but for his
grand mind."

"And Clärchen?"

"Says the world has no happiness equal to
that of being Egmont's beloved."

"Clärchen was not Egmont's wife?"

"Oh, no; she was merely a girl whom he
loved."

"That accounts for their affection. If they
had been married they would have wrangled
and jangled, just like any other respectable
married couple."

"Then the play becomes sad," continues
Thyrza. "Alba is jealous of Egmont's renown
and plots against him and entraps him. You
see him ride up to the Duke's palace on his

favourite horse—such a pet! he dismounts and passes his hand lovingly over its mane. Alba, all the while, is looking on from a window above, and in another moment his generous foe has gone mirthfully, unsuspectingly to his fate. Alba offers Egmont his life if he will change his principles. And Egmont, though so fond of living, will not be saved at the expense of his honour. Poor Clärchen! She tries to save him, but what can a little peasant girl do? After she hears the news Egmont is to die, the scene opens in her cottage again. She enters with a lighted lamp in her hand, which, as it is the only light in the theatre, shows out distinctly. But, ah! what is the use of telling you, monsieur? You will laugh and say it is foolish sentiment," interrupting herself, and whisking the heads off several unoffending daisies with her whip.

"I can assure you I am deeply interested, mademoiselle," returns Ferrier. "I can guess how the play ends. Egmont, at the last moment, when his head is on the block, escapes. Clärchen and he are married, and live happy ever after."

"No. Well, she places the lamp in the window, to let Brackenburg see she waits for him. He is a burgher and her devoted lover.

Presently he comes, and she hears there is no hope of rescuing Egmont. Then she poisons herself; and Egmont, as he lies sleeping, sees the spirit of Clärchen holding a crown of laurels over his head. He goes to die as the sun rises and the dawn spreads over the sky, and the Platz is illumined by its rays. It was splendid!" drawing a long breath.

"What sort of a life can you have had to take so much interest in a man who has been dead long ago?"

"I have been happy enough. Then after the play we had a grand supper in the back room, where M. Paul and madame make wigs, and plaits, and curls, and cushions for the hair. They send quantities over to London."

"You'll spoil your complexion," says Ferrier, abruptly. "Why don't you put on your hat?"

"Oh, there is no fear of spoiling my complexion," she laughs. "It would be impossible to do that. I am so brown already that a little more sunburn does not matter—and then I don't freckle, which is a good thing. Freckles are *so* ugly."

"I am rather partial to freckles," he returns. "They are generally the sign of a smooth skin. All young ladies ought to take care of their complexion; part of their stock-in-trade, you know."

"But I am not a young lady."

"What are you then? A female?"

"Oh, hateful word!" she rejoins, indignantly.

"Woman, spelt in capitals? No? Perhaps you would wish to be termed a young person? No, again? Well, I'm blest if I know, and it is too hot to-day to exercise one's brains much," stretching himself along the parapet lazily. "Oh, my prophetic soul, it *is* hot! Jove! You'll not find it very cheerful at Carmylie. There are only the fisher folks in the way of society."

"But I shall see you, shall I not?" says she, naïvely.

"Why, yes, if it is conducive to your happiness, you'll see me pretty often, as we are going to live in the same house for the next year."

"A year?—twelve whole months?"

"It will soon go, mademoiselle. Are not you sorry that, instead of 'coming out,' as girls generally do at your age, you have got to work? I daresay you have moaned over the parties and fineries you have lost."

"You see I never knew what they were like, and one cannot miss what one has never had. I was brought up to work, and I am not ashamed of it. There is nothing but what is honourable in work, and I have got a pair of hands."

" Let's have a look at this pair of hands that are so able and willing to work."

Thyrza pulls off her gloves, and Ferrier takes her slender fingers into his own broad palm.

" No rings?" he asked, interrogatively ; " indeed, no earrings, either ?"

" No, I don't like them."

" By-and-by, some one will come and put a band of plain gold round this little thifd finger of the left hand, and you will promise to be faithful and true, and will follow his fortunes over the world. So you are going to earn your own livelihood with these morsels of hands ? Why, I could break them to bits. Don't move them away. I have a curiosity to look at them. How brown and sunburned they are !"

" Matching my face," she replies, gravely and simply.

" This is the line of life, here is the line of fortune, and there is the line of intellect. Properly you ought to give the fortune-teller a piece of money to cross your palm with. Have you any with you ?"

" No, I have none."

" This will do as well," feeling in his pocket

for a sovereign among some loose coins. Then he crosses her hand with the gold, Thyrza not laughing or giggling, but looking on very quietly and calmly.

"Monsieur, move the pony's head. He is going to eat my flowers. I think some time or other I should like to be a nurse in a hospital. Madame Paul took me over the hospital of S. Sulpice at Villios. The Sisters of Charity had such calm, quiet, holy faces, with no earthly passions imprinted on them. When—oh, monsieur, what are you doing to my hands?"

"Reading your fortune from the lines. Go on, mademoiselle. When——"

"When I am tired of the world, I shall go there, I think."

"And give Heaven the dregs of your life, after the freshness and innocence have been rubbed off. A real woman's creed that—coquette while that amusement can be practised, then dévote for the rest of the time. But you were never fitted for S. Sulpice. To begin with, you would have all the fellows breaking their legs and arms to be nursed by you, of which little game the good Sisters would not approve, and you would be continually in hot water : you were meant to be a man's companion, and not to go through life single file."

" If I was loved as Egmont loved Clärchen, I should not mind any amount of suffering afterwards."

" That is to say, for a few hours of perfect happiness, you would endure a life of misery. A dangerous idea for a man; a doubly dangerous one for a woman. There, mademoiselle," relinquishing her hands, " I read long life and moderate fortune. Don't have that foolish notion any longer in your mind. There is one law for the man by which he always comes off scot free, and another for the woman by which she is without fail condemned. That thought of yours is precisely what leads people to the bad."

" To the bad ?" she inquires.

" Don't you understand me ? It signifies betting and racing, and gambling, and spending money on everything we ought not to spend it on, generally winding up with not a penny to bless oneself with, and a ruined constitution."

" Did you ever do that, monsieur ?"

" Well, there are not many things I have not had a try at in my time, and I wish now I had let a few of them alone."

" Ah, but what would it signify if I went to the bad ?" says she, defiantly. " Who would cry for me, or put on mourning if I died to-morrow? I am of as much importance in the world as this spray of mountain-ash flower," rising and throwing into the river a tuft of rowan blossoms.

"You don't know what you are talking about," returns Ferrier. "It is absurd to say it would not matter. I, for one, should be sorry to see a girl like you—I don't say a *nice* girl, but simply a girl like you—spoil her future, when it lies with herself to make it a prosperous one."

He is careful not to praise, nor to flatter, nor to compliment her in any one way, as she stands leaning over the broad low parapet, her hat in her hand, the dark blue habit falling in graceful curves round her slim figure, her face and eyes glowing with life, looking pretty enough in the wavering tesselated lights and shadows to have tempted S. Anthony himself to forswear celibacy and his hermit's cell. There is a long pause; Thyzra is silent. The lowing of the oxen; the hum of insect life; the chirping of the birds; the roar of the river from the rough waters, make music on the ear in the sultry hush of the sun-steeped, hot midsummer day. There is not a breath of air stirring: the wind is too lazy to waft the perfume of the meadow down from the opposite side of the stream, or break the rainbow tinted foam bubbles at the sandy margin by the arum lilies. The spray of rowan flower floats like a feather in mid-air, hovering gently above the bog, by the grim grey kelpie's head, in whose grinning mouth a fern has taken root and is growing luxuriantly; then it slowly descends on to the water's surface, where it is caught by contrary currents from sundry tiny cascades of mountain burns, running down the red sandstone rocks to the river from the hills. It sails along smoothly under the shadow of the ivy-clad trees, gets into trouble and threatens to be swamped when the bed becomes rough and rocky, almost becalmed by a shelving promontory, is righted by a faint puff of wind, and finally is borne peacefully and tranquilly out of sight upon the bosom of a deep pool.

" The poor little tempest-tossed bark has got safely into port," says Ferrier, at length. " I watched it with some anxiety."

" Monsieur, what time is it, please ?" she asks, somewhat sharply.

" Not quite three o'clock."

" I must go back to Lillieshill now."

" I am going there too."

" There is a short way by a path along the river side. It is impossible for monsieur to miss it."

" I intend to accompany mademoiselle on the

road to Lillieshill. Did you want to get rid of me?"

"I thought monsieur was tired of my society," says she, candidly, "so do not come out of civility to me. I can go home by myself."

"It suits me better to walk with you," he returns, quietly. "How about mounting? Will the pony stand while I put you up?"

"I don't think he will. But if you will hold his head I will get on myself."

Ferrier brings the pony closer to the parapet, on which Thyrza, her habit gathered round her, is standing. She runs along a few yards, and is preparing to give a jump of delight, when Ferrier drags her down by both wrists, and catching her in his arms, lifts her bodily on to the pony.

"Are you mad?" he cries, grasping the reins, while Thryza hits June Rose sharply on the off flank, making the half-thoroughbred mare rear and plunge. "I never saw such insensate folly. Perhaps you think it *fine* and *spirited* to show off like that?"

"Monsieur, you have taken an *unpardonable* liberty," she says, with flashing eyes.

"You took an unpardonable liberty with your-self. One step backwards and you would have been killed. It made me giddy to look at you, and if you had fallen over, I should have been had up for manslaughter."

" Pouf!" rejoins Thyrza, with a gay laugh. "And if it had been, it is only death at the worst. A hundred years hence, when two or three old bones are all that remain of me, it will not matter whether I broke my neck or lived to threescore and ten. It is all the same in the end. One must die sooner or later. Only I should like to enjoy myself, and have a little fun first."

Ferrier slackens the reins, and she and he go up the hill together towards Lillieshill, the small terrier trotting behind them.

CHAPTER VII.

I DON'T like to hear you talk in that fool-hardy way," resumes Ferrier, when they have climbed the brae, and are upon the high road. "It is—how shall I say it?—not proper conversation for a young lady."

"That is just why I hate being a girl," returns Thyrza. "If I had been a man I should not have been bothered about the proprieties, and sitting up pretty all day long, and behaving myself like a *young lady*." The last words she pronounces with intense disgust. "Bah! If I had been a man I could have gone into commerce abroad."

"I might have taken you out to China with me as a clerk. What a pity you are not a boy!"

"Is it not? I suppose it would not do to dress up in man's clothes and cut my hair short? No one would ever find it out."

"No, *hardly*," says Ferrier, biting the corners

of his lips to restrain his laughter. What an innocent little thing she is, unless she puts it on ; if she does, it certainly does credit to her stage powers. " Well, go in for being a lady medical—Dr. Thyrza Rutherfurd, M.D. ! How would that sound ? Ah ! I forgot. You have no nerve. If you could not help me to bandage the Italian lad's head, how would you face the dissecting rooms ? But, of course, you will marry. Have you ever thought about that ?"

" Occasionally, monsieur. But I don't think I shall. The person I liked might not care for me, and I would never marry unless I was very fond of the man. Besides, who would marry a plain penniless girl like me ?"

" Ah, to be sure, it is not probable. Money and beauty are such essentials. What do you mean by ' being fond ' of a person ?"—giving a look of admiration in spite of himself at the outlines of Thyrza's figure, showing clear against the brilliant blue sky.

" Oh ! loving with heart and soul, better than everyone and everything else in the world."

" Charming in theory, the reverse in practice. For how long ?"

" For ever."

" What is your definition of ' for ever.' Until next month ?"

" No, all one's life."

"What would you do for a person you loved?
Cut off your hair? I know you are proud of it.
The Chinese mandarin with the red ball would
make it into a famous pigtail."

" Cut off my hair !" she repeats, scornfully ;
" I would cut off my *foot* if it were necessary."

" You might find it inconvenient to go through
life with only one foot. Your hair, teeth, complexion, youth, are so many valuable articles in
the marriage market ; as you lose them, your
value decreases. But could you put up with
the vagaries and fads of a jealous person ?"

" If he loved me, and I loved him, yes."

" How do you know the person would be *he ?*
It might be an old maid with the orthodox
cat."

" I took it for granted."

" Mademoiselle Thyrza, I pity you !" says
Ferrier.

" Why ?" she asks, astonished.

" You are so completely devoid of common
sense and prudence. Your head is stuffed full
of romance and sentiment. Common sense is a
better gift than genius; with it, and tact as
ballast, you will get along easily. Love, such as
you describe it, does not exist ; it is an exploded
notion. Two asses—don't be offended—two de-

luded asses swearing vows to adore each other to all eternity, belong to a past generation."

" It was a much nicer one, monsieur."

" No, we are far wiser. Love now-a-days is resolvable into the amount of pounds, shillings and pence a man or woman is prepared to bid in exchange for a bundle of silk, frivolity, simpering nothingness, false hair, rouge, pearl-powder and feminine spite, or conglomeration of Poole's clothes, ambition, vanity, which go to make up a belle or dandy of the first water. If a little genuine liking can be thrown into the bargain, all the better."

" If I don't meet my ideal, I shall never marry."

" You are worse off than the bundle of silk ; for you seem to have ideas of your own."

" I wish I could do as I liked."

" Well, suppose you can, let me hear the result."

" Make myself very pretty."

" Oh, come now, you don't expect me to believe you think yourself ugly. It's a nice opportunity for paying a compliment; but I never pay compliments."

" That must be as you like, monsieur. I should have golden hair and blue eyes———"

" And a complexion like the wax model in a

barber's shop. I abominate fair women. They are generally vicious, with vile tempers, and either become dried up and shrivelled after thirty, or else inordinately stout."

" Monsieur admires dark people then ?"

" I admire a pretty fair woman and a pretty dark woman; it's all the same to me, as long as they are good-looking. I don't object to something *rich* and *dark*," glancing at Thyrza's pomegranate cheeks; " but most of all I admire a *sensible* woman."

" Why ?"

" Because they are so seldom seen."

" Oh, I should like to do something really *worth* doing."

" Much better cultivate the art of dressing and restrain your imagination. It never pays. Allow me to follow out your theory of love in a cottage. How would you like to bring up a large family on next to nothing? Think of the realities ; maid-of-all-work in shoes down at heels and slatternly gown; continual smell of soapsuds about the house ; children in chronic state of toothache: I think you would then prefer love in the *abstract*, as the discreet Edinburgh damsel said.

" I *am* glad I am not your wife," exclaims

Thyrza, " but if she had any of your favourite quality, common sense, she would keep you in order."

" Are you ?" says Ferrier, much amused. " But don't distress yourself on my account. I shall *never* have a wife for two reasons. I don't believe in women, and if I did, I can't afford to marry. But if you *were* my wife, you would be a good little thing, and sew on my shirt buttons, and fill my pipe with tobacco if I were too tired or too lazy to do it for myself."

" Not I," says Thyrza, tossing her head. " I should do nothing of the kind. I should cut holes in your stockings, and leave you to stitch them up yourself."

" No, you would not," persists Ferrier, finding it impossible to resist laughing :—the more he laughs, the glummer Thyrza looks—" although that is what we are coming to; but it wont be quite in my day. Now, mademoiselle, I'll prove to you in three words that if you and I were husband and wife you would do exactly what I told you. Please to suppose for a minute that we *are* married and are Mr. and Mrs. Ferrier. Did not you say a moment ago that you would marry no one unless you loved him, heart and soul ?"

"Well, yes, monsieur," answers Thyrza, hesitatingly, unable to deny her own assertion.

"And that if you loved him you would do *any*thing for him—would not even stick at cutting off hair or foot, if necessary ? Consequently, if you married me you would love me intensely, and if you would perform such heroic and out-of-the-way actions, you could not refuse the little commonplace ones I have mentioned."

"Mais, monsieur——"

"I will give you an example of what it would be. If we were married, I should call you Thyrza and you would call me Jack."

"Mais oui, c'est vrai, Monsieur Jacques. Well, it is a fact; looking at it, of course, in the light monsieur suggests."

"Of course," says Ferrier, "in the imaginary light. But if you were Mrs. Ferrier you would not say *monsieur*, but simply Jack. Confound that dog Wasp, he's always up to some mischief !"

Wasp, seeing one of his detested and arch enemies—a cat—bolts after it across the road into a cottage, upsetting two fat children in his excited movements, who immediately set up a direful squall. He stumbles up against an old woman engaged in the occupation of winding *pirns*, and stands on the very points of his hind heels

barking and growling, with every hair on his
body quivering with emotion and exasperation,
while the cat has taken refuge on the mantel-
shelf, having knocked down an image of the
Duke of Wellington in china, on a fearfully
and wonderfully prancing horse, which is thereby
smashed to atoms. Out comes the old woman
in white mutch, red and black checked shawl
crossed over her chest, and grey linsey woolsey
petticoat, to the door, picks up the unlucky
infants, bestowing hearty cuffs upon them by
way of cheering them a little, and pours forth
a volley of abuse at Ferrier in the very broadest
Lowland Scotch, which is complete gibberish to
both Thyrza and himself. From within pro-
ceed sounds of snarls and growls ; the cat is
spitting and swearing ad libitum ; Wasp has got
on the top of the chest of drawers and is within
an ace of touching the cat's whiskers. It is a
stupendous moment of excitement for Wasp ; but
just as he makes a snap at puss, which she
catfully parries by a vicious dab at his black
nose, Ferrier brings his triumph to an untimely
end, by catching him and lifting him down by
the scruff of his neck. It is a primitive little
cottage of two rooms, a *but* and a *ben*, containing dark, close box-beds. The floor is earthen,
without any pretence at boards ; some flaring

Scripture prints and cheap valentines hang over the mantelpiece; bannocks are baking on a girdle over a peat fire; the rafters are filled with newspapers; bags of onions; fishing-rods; a couple of guns, and besides seem apparently to be the receptacles for the family clothing. A cuckoo-clock ticks away in one corner, its hands creeping slowly over its old, faded, painted face, and a big Bible in a print cover is on the window-sill. The spinning-wheel, at which the woman was working, stands at the fireside, and a box of *pirns* or large reels of yarn lies on the floor.

"What is your name?" asks Ferrier, as she is obliged to draw to a close from sheer want of breath.

"Margaret Gow," is the reply.

"Well, here's half-a-crown for you," says Ferrier. "On whose property do you live?"

"Carmylie," she returns, considerably pacified. "And it's a sair job I hae to gaither the baw-bees till the rent, and that's true, sir. This is an awfu' uncanny hoose, and sic cauld winds i' the winter, and me sic troubled wi' the rheumatics and near dead wi' the teeth ache."

"Well, I'll think over what can be done about giving you a better floor."

"The lord keep me! and will you be the new

Laird of Carmylie? Preserve us a', and me gieing you yer kail through the reek that gait. He's a bonny bit beast that," endeavouring to pat Wasp, who is delivering certain parting growls of defiance, and scratching up the dust with his feet. But Wasp refuses the overtures of peace, and keeps close at Ferrier's heels. As they move away the man who unloosened the horse from the cart at the bridge appears with the said cart and draws up at Gow's cottage. He is a tall, powerfully built man, six feet two or three in height, with shoulders like those of a Hercules; his face is slightly marked with small-pox, and he has the peculiarity of only possessing one arm.

"I believe that fellow is one of the biggest poachers for miles round," exclaims Ferrier. "I never knew his name before, but I suspect he is the son of that delightful Margaret Gow, and those are his wife and children welcoming him home. How he gets his living is a mystery to me; chiefly by eating his neighbour's game, I am told."

"Now, Mrs. Ferrier," continues Jack, "where did I leave off in our little conversation? You must try to think that we are married, and living, shall we say in London? I am in business and come home at night, done up with the day's work. After dinner I say, Thyrza dear, will you hand me the tobacco? I am sure you would not refuse. Any one whom you love would be your master. Can you love intensely?" laying his hand on the reins of the pony and stopping it.

"No, monsieur, I don't believe I could," she answers saucily. "I shall leave that for the man to do."

"Oh, you story-telling girl, when you have been admiring the devotion of Clärchen for Egmont! That's the way with you, is it—say one thing and believe another? But there, mademoiselle, I wish you a better fate than to marry a man like me. I'll tell you what; take my advice and go in for an eligible. You are coming to our place. I'll ask a few down in the autumn for you to choose from."

"I shan't go in for anyone," replies Thyrza. "If they like to go in for me all well and good."

"There spoke sweet seventeen. At that period you say, who shall I have? When you are thirty-seven instead of seventeen, you will wish you had gone in for the eligibles."

"Never: better be an old maid a hundred thousand times over than lose one's self-respect by marrying a man whom one did not love."

"You will find self-respect a poor substitute

for the support of a husband's affection when all your friends and schoolfellows have settled down comfortable in the world with their families, and you are necessary to the happiness of no one. A woman, at least a nice-minded woman, lives chiefly in her affections. It is all very well to hold those opinions in the bloom and spring-time of your life. You should listen to the experiences of a grey-headed man like me."

"Oh, bother the future!" says Thyrza, smiling; her dark face dimpling with pleasure. "Perhaps I shan't live to be old and ugly. I am sure I shall be a hideous old woman, dark persons do not make such pretty old people as fair ones do. That is another advantage men have; their looks don't signify at all."

"Consolation for me," returns Ferrier. "If I had a wife she should be a calm dignified woman of unruffled demeanour; exquisitely beautiful, that is a *sine quâ non*; she must know the price of everything; be accomplished; always know the right thing; be an angel of amiability; always well dressed," with a mischievous glance at Thyrza's collar, which is, as usual, crooked.

"Monsieur desires perfection."

"Yes, that is why I shall never marry. My

beau ideal is not in the flesh.   But, after all, there's nothing equal to a faithful friend—

> "And, of all best things upon earth, I hold that a
>   faithful friend is the best,
> For woman, Will, is a thorny flower; it breaks, and
>   we bleed and smart."

Do you know the rest, mademoiselle?"

"Monsieur quoting poetry?" asks Thyrza, in surprise.

"A slip of the tongue, *lapsus linguæ*, as it used to say in the old Eton grammar."

"We turn in here," says Thyrza, pausing at a newly painted green gate, and trim lodge built in imitation of a Swiss chalet, with balconies running round the front, and lattice windows designed more for their picturesque appearance than the purpose of admitting light and air into the dwelling.

"Seriously," pursues Ferrier, "you should cultivate Mark.   He is a real good fellow as ever stepped the ground, sound in all points, and free from vice.   He does not even smoke too much."

Thyrza shakes her head.   "I am a born old maid."

"I have found you out, mademoiselle."

"How?"

" You talk for *effect*."

" It was rather fun to shock you by making you think I was fast," she replies, " you did look so scandalized and horrified. I used to delight in telling Miss Holt all sorts of things. But here are Mr. Mark and Mr. Lefroy. If you want to win Mr. Lefroy's heart, praise the lodge and say you noticed the elegant contrivance of the pivot on which the hinge of the gate turns. It is ' entirely his own design.' "

" Well, Jack, glad to see you again. So you have come at last," says Mark, shaking hands heartily with Ferrier. " I began to think that you had stuck in the middle of the Suez Canal."

" I am very glad to be back in England too. I should have been home sooner had it not been that the engines of the steamer got out of order. But I had a nice little continental tour and took it easy."

" How long have you been travelling altogether ?" asks Mr. Lefroy.

" Nearly four months ; but then the vessel broke down, and we were a number of weeks in Bombay, besides my trip through Italy and France."

" Did you walk from Carmylie ? It must have been warm work."

" Well, rather. I lost my way half a dozen

times by taking wrong turnings at cross-roads. Are there *no* sign-posts in Scotland?"

" Not in the neighbourhood of Lillieshill."

" We have only two lumbering carriage horses at Carmylie, which *the* man and general help informed me were engaged in some carting about the fields. There remaining only an old pony, I preferred walking to breaking my neck. Good people are scarce, you know."

" Just so," says Mr. Lefroy.

" How did the ponies I bought for you in London turn out, Mark?"

" Let me give you a word of warning, Mr. Ferrier."

" Yes?" inquires Ferrier of Mr. Lefroy.

" Never be the person to buy a horse for a friend, and never commission a friend to buy one for you. It's never safe."

" Oh! I don't know about that," breaks in Mark, " it may do very well as a general rule, but it does not apply to Ferrier and me."

" That's a nicish animal Mademoiselle is on," observes Ferrier, examining its fetlocks, with the light coming into his eyes, which is only seen in an Englishman's when looking at a particularly choice specimen of horse flesh, " would make a good lady's hunter."

" Yes, wouldn't it?" replies Mark, pleased at

Ferrier's approbation. Few things gratify a man more than to praise his judgment regarding horses.

"You've picked up riding rather quickly, mademoiselle," says Ferrier, with a critical glance at Thyrza's easy seat.

"Yes, thanks to Mr. Mark. It has been such a treat. I never knew what *living* meant until I rode June Rose."

"You must have been pretty well employed, what with painting and riding."

"We had nothing else to do, had we, Miss Thyrza? I feel like a fish out of water without my business to attend to, and read the money market list in the papers just out of sheer force of habit. Nice clean high action, has she not?"

"Yes, steps out well, and lifts her feet cleverly from the ground."

"I see you are a chip of the old block, Mr. Ferrier," pursues Mr. Lefroy. "There was nothing Mr. Ferrier of Carmylie liked better than to look over a lot of horses."

"Ah, yes," responds Jack, "the poor old governor had a good eye for a horse."

"Well, Mr. Ferrier, Luke and I were going to have a look at the cattle before you came. I dare say you don't trouble yourself about anything in the agricultural line, or else it would give me great pleasure to show you my model cowhouse."

"By-the-by, Miss Thyrza, would you like to dismount now? I'll take June Rose to the stables for you as Smith is not here."

Thyrza gives her horse to Mark, and Ferrier having no objection to urge, Mr. Lefroy leads the way to his pet hobby, after a brief delay, occasioned by the absence of Mark.

The situation of the model cowhouse has been carefully chosen; it is on a dry sheltered spot, facing the south. The material used for building is brick; the roof is of variegated coloured slates. The windows are lancet-shaped, like those of a church or chapel, for which the cowhouse has occasionally been mistaken, and they are of stained glass. The walls are painted pink, with ventilators in the ceiling. Pipes put all round provide for heating the place in the winter, and the fittings are of polished pine wood. The animals are perfect of their sort; gazelle-eyed Alderney cows, almost as graceful in their proportions as deer; sleek, hornless, "Angus doddies," Ayrshire, and other varieties. The cattle intended for the forthcoming agricultural show in England are in another division of the building; they are all of one kind, the black Angus.

"That fellow there," says Mr. Lefroy, indicating a noble young bull, black as night, with fiery eyes, beginning to show signs of restlessness at the presence of strangers, "is going up to Battersea by-and-by. He will have his coat laid in butter-milk for a fortnight beforehand, and will travel in a padded carriage, with two men to look after him."

"He is a beauty and no mistake," answers Jack, feeling called upon to make some observation.

"I am always remarkably brave when there is a barrier between myself and the danger," says Mark, laughing, while Mr. Lefroy is engaged in showing the good points and breeding of the animal, and relating how he made more than two hundred pounds in prize money the year before.

"I remember," remarks Ferrier—"I remember reading an account in the English newspapers some years ago of the rinderpest, which devastated the country. Did you lose any cattle then?"

"No, curiously enough, I never lost one."

"You were more fortunate then than most people. What do you think your exemption was owing to?"

"I never allowed any stranger to enter the cowhouse. Indeed, if her Majesty Queen Victoria herself had begged me to allow her, I should have said, that though as loyal a subject as her Majesty possesses, I could not consent to her entrance. Then I kept up the system of the cattle; gave them oilcake and the best of food, while my neighbours weakened the constitution of theirs by arsenicum and other disinfecting stuff. An acquaintance of mine who reared the best Angus cattle I ever saw—excepting my own—built a hospital in readiness and doctored the poor animals; he lost *every* head, and he took it so to heart that he was never the same man afterwards. A small farmer close by where he lived made no attempt at any precautions, and like myself never had a single animal attacked by the disease. Remarkable, very, was it not?"

"Very remarkable!" responds Jack. "That fellow looks as though he had a little temper of his own."

"Oh, not in the least, I assure you," says Mr. Lefroy, gazing with the rapt eyes of a fond lover at the black Angus. "Jupiter is mild as a lamb. He is too fat to be ill-natured. Come, Jupiter, look up, there's a pretty dear, and let Miss Rutherfurd pat you."

In testimony of his meek qualities, Jupiter puts his head between his knees, and lashes his sides with his tail, giving a tremendous roar, and endeavours to paw the ground but is unable to make much of this, the floor being paved with encaustic tiles.

" Well, Mr. Ferrier," observes Mr. Lefroy complacently, regarding the cowhouse, which has cost him a long way over the tidy sum of a thousand pounds, with its pointed pepper-box turrets and its Gothic windows, " I do not say it ostentatiously or presumptuously, but MY cowhouse is the best in the three kingdoms ; " and, after a brief pause, he adds, with a sigh of perfect, unalloyed bliss, his cup of happiness being filled to the brim, " there is no doubt about it."

" No one can dispute that," says Mark. " Come now, Jack, we will go down to the house. You must want pulling together, and I can give uncle's sherry a good character. It has been to India and back to season it."

" Ah, you'll not beat my sherry in all Scotland, Mr. Ferrier. You had better bring the dog with you into the drawing-room. I have just had the place newly painted from top to toe, and if you leave him outside he'll scrape all the paint off the door," chimes in Mr. Lefroy, who is always ready to sing his own praises, and though one of the vainest, is also one of the best tempered of men.

Lillieshill is looking its best when they reach the front door ; the warm sunshine gilding the old house and its " ivy-green ;" the close shaven velvet lawn, studded with flower-beds of scarlet geraniums, yellow calceolarias, blue lobelias, and verbenas, and ribbon-borders of every tint, all out in the most brilliant bloom, while some peacocks strut along, spreading out their iris-hued tails like fans for the admiration, according to the Darwinian theory, of their assembled partners and families.

Afternoon tea is set out on a small three-legged table in the conservatory, into which Mr. Lefroy escorts Ferrier, through a door opening on the lawn, for the express convenience, Mr. Lefroy declares, of burglars and other light-fingered members of society.

" Thyrza dear, will you pour out tea ?" asks Miss Lefroy. " I feel rather tired with my morning wanderings."

Thyrza at once complies, and Mark makes himself serviceable in handing the cups. As he stands beside Thyrza by a tall New Zealand fern under an arch of crimson Virginia-creeper hanging in thick flowers and curving tendrils, Jack thinks what a well-matched couple they are ; he fair and she dark. A good contrast to each other, and Mark is just the right age for Thyrza.

Mark, it is true, is older than Jack by some three or four years, but Ferrier always feels considerably the elder of the two.

Jack regards his friend almost tenderly; his true and faithful friend after the lapse of many years, from boyhood to manhood; no change in the steady real affection which has grown up with time to be solid and enduring as the beautiful friendship of David and Jonathan. He knows that whatever trouble or evil hours may come upon him there will always be a warm corner in Luke Mark's heart for Jack Ferrier; he knows that though the whole world should turn against him, this friend will always welcome him, believe in him, swear to his honour and to his truth, and put complete and absolute trust in him. All else may turn to gall and bitterness; all else change; all else forsake him, yet Mark, the companion of his schoolboy pleasures and escapades, of his shooting expeditions for big game up the country in China; of his business speculations in Shanghai, will cleave to him: will—should occasion require such assistance—spend his last pound to help him out of his difficulty. Jack is certain of all this, for he has proved it. He has not a thought but what is shared with Mark; there is nothing underhand about Jack. Sooner than "keep things dark,"

or live like Damocles with a sword hanging over
his head, he would endure any pain, however
severe it might be at the time, and plain-speaking
is one of the attributes which has often made
him eremics and got him into trouble. Mark
he considers fantastic in many of his notions:
was it not peculiar for a young man of three
and twenty to adopt an orphan as Mark had
done? Most men of that age prefer to spend
their money in wild oats and upon themselves.
But then it was one of Mark's fancies, which
expression to Ferrier, who imagines he knows
every shade and turn of Luke's face and character,
accounts for any outbreak. From the first he had,
so to speak, looked after Mark. If Luke got
into scrapes at school, Jack most frequently bore
the blame; if Mark had an imposition to write,
Jack usually wrote the greater part, and read the
remainder aloud for Mark's benefit. If Jack
had a " grub-box " from home—they were like
angels' visits, few and far between, for Jack was
little thought of save as a tiresome lad who must
be clothed and fed—Mark got the lion's share.
Jack fought Mark's battles for him, punched the
heads of those who attempted to tyrannize over
the somewhat weakly and delicate boy, and was
rarely without the ornament of a black eye,
gained in Mark's defence. Mark, on his part,

spoiled by his indulgent uncle and aunt at Lillieshill, made much of and adored at every turn, took all Jack's services as his right and a matter of course. He munched· Jack's tarts and spent his sixpences right royally; next to his mother, Ferrier was most deeply attached to Mark. When they grew up and went out to Shanghai, the younger, still as formerly, apparently led, and in reality got the roughest of the work. Mark did not desire to give dross in exchange for gold, which is, ah! such a common bargain; his purse is always open to Jack if he wishes, and he values Ferrier's good opinion more than that of any other living man. Jack's standard of right and wrong is that to which Mark pins his faith and swears by. He has only one secret from Jack, and that one is the existence of Lilith Mark. If Jack knew of the deception that has been practised on him by his most intimate friend for years : if he guessed that Lilith was Mark's wife, away would go all their friendship, all the pleasant hours they had spent over their pipes and B. and S.'s; there would be no more fishing, and shooting, and riding together. Jack would never forgive the fraud; over and over again Mark has heard him say he could forgive anything excepting meanness and deceit; he would simply not speak to him again, and would cut him dead.

However, this disagreeable idea need not be contemplated, for by no chance nor possibility can Jack ever find out, unless Thyrza betrays him, and he has settled that matter to his entire satisfaction, so he is quite safe and there is no fear of it leaking out.

" Miss Lefroy, can anyone be handsome who is *freckled ?*" asks Thyrza abruptly, pouring out another cup of tea for Mark. Of all domestic avocations there are not many so pretty and becoming to a woman as that one of making tea. The attitude of raising the arm to lift the tea-pot shows off waist and bust to advantage, and if ordinarily good-looking and possessed of a tolerable figure, almost any girl will look charming at the head of her table, more especially when the table is a little round three-legged one, and the background is of Virginia-creeper. Then, afternoon tea has none of the formality about it that appertains to the late dinner; there are such convenient opportunities for bewitchingly simple costumes ; and how much can be made out of handing a cup of tea, and the apparently innocent question of whether you take both cream and sugar? Hardly anybody does now-a-days, but it is wonderful what an aid towards cementing intimacy the discovery of similarity of tastes even in so small a thing as cream or sugar may be. One of the pleasantest hours of the day in a country house is when every one assembles for afternoon tea. It is agreeable in the autumn to sit in a corner that was evidently created by the various architects of Lillieshill for " spoony " people, and talk nonsense over tea and thin bread and butter, or the delicious sponge cake which almost melts in your mouth, made by Mr. Lefroy's sovereign and paragon of cooking excellence, the Lillieshill cook; or to lounge in the summer under one of the fine old beech trees which have charitably been provided with massive and wide trunks, while the rooks caw odd songs to each other, which, though discordant and noisy in our ears, may yet sound very melodious to Mrs. or Miss Rook.

" Freckles ! " says Miss Lefroy, " no, my dear, I should think not."

" Mr. Ferrier said he thought they were very pretty."

" Oh no," rejoins Ferrier, laughing, " I merely said I rather liked them."

" Do you know any one with freckles, Jack ? The only person I ever knew who admired them was a man who told me he was partial to freckles and red hair, and besides that he rather affected

squints.   It afterwards turned out he was engaged to a girl who squinted and he married
her.   Jack clearly intends to marry a squinting
young woman with lots of freckles and a meagre
supply of light sandy hair."

"Oh, nonsense, Mark.   I don't mean to
marry.   I think I see myself going up the
church aisle to execution, with my face very
long and pale, my step slow—I should go as
slowly as I could—and my hands crossed in
front as if they were handcuffed."

"It would be a poor compliment to the bride
to be welcomed by a lugubrious bridegroom."

"I wish Carmylie was in anything like the
order in which you have Lillieshill," pursues
Ferrier.   "My poor father's death occurred so
suddenly and so soon after that of my brother
that all energy seems to have been knocked out
of my mother, and things have been left to take
care of themselves."

"Ah, I pique myself a little about Lillieshill,"
returns Mr. Lefroy; "but I manage the farm
and garden entirely on my own plan, and though
I say it myself, you will not find a place in
Europe or America better arranged.   It is particularly well managed; particularly so."

"I am disappointed in Carmylie.   No doubt
it looked better when properly kept, yet I can

hardly fancy how my father could have preferred it to Blackbeck in Lincolnshire."

"He only lived there during the shooting season, and he liked it because it was near moors swarming with grouse. After the 10th of December he went down to Melton Mowbray for the hunting. But certainly Carmylie is not the house it was during your father's lifetime."

"I don't believe the game is anything particular, and the villagers poach in broad daylight and think nothing of it. That William Gow coolly walks through the avenue as a short cut to the preserves. The keeper is afraid of him, and so he goes unmolested."

"I know the man," says Mr. Lefroy, with interest, "comes of a shocking bad lot. He was a *Pendicler*—that is, his ancestors got the land their cottage is built on rent free, in consideration of reclaiming some fields from the heather. Gow pays only a nominal rent. Originally these pendiclers were of the very scum of the earth —the off-scourings of creation."

"Well, Gow has a rascally countenance; but he has a stunning figure."

"He loafs about the country, sometimes hawking pedlar's goods, and sometimes he drives a fish cadger's cart. I know he poaches in the

Lillieshill woods, but I've never been able to get hold of him."

"Is this a sociable neighbourhood, Miss Lefroy?" asks Jack, turning to her. "It seems a thinly-populated one as regards cottages. I don't think I passed above a dozen on my way here."

"There are plenty of gentlemen's seats, but very few of the owners live in them. When they are inhabited, it is almost always only in the shooting season, and then they are tenanted by rich English merchants. Country houses are very expensive things to keep up properly, especially if you live any distance from a town. How far is Carmylie from Queensmuir?"

"A little more than twelve miles."

"That is a long way from a post-town. Carmylie is a dear place to live in, and the grounds and garden alone would require a small fortune expended on them in the shape of gardeners and under-gardeners. It must be very awkward having to send such a distance for your letters and household groceries. How do you manage about your coals?"

"The farmers have a clause inserted in their leases whereby they are compelled, so many times a year, to cart coals from Queensmuir to Carmylie."

"Something of the kind is quite necessary. In winter you will be obliged to lay in a store of provisions, for the road through the glen is sometimes blocked up with snow and is quite impassable for weeks. But perhaps you will not remain over the winter with Mrs. Ferrier."

"That I cannot tell at present; but certainly not if I can help it."

"Mrs. Ferrier, I daresay, feels nervous occasionally, being so far distant in case of emergency from a medical man. We are better off in that respect at Lillieshill, for we are only six miles from Queensmuir, and we think nothing of that. You have had a sad home-coming, Mr. Ferrier. We were so sorry to lose your father and brother, both such fine hale handsome men too."

"It has not been what I looked forward to," returns Ferrier, briefly.

The spirit moves Mr. Lefroy to offer some consoling observation to Jack, but he does not know in what terms to couch his sympathy. If it had been Jupiter or Europa seized with pneumonia, he would have found plenty to say. But this is such a different subject, and one in which his feelings and his heart are not so absorbed.

"Bless me! dear me! dear me! It is indeed a melancholy thing, very, particularly so. But you know these—eh! hum!—these little accidents will happen, and one cannot prevent them!"

"Very true," answers Jack, moving to show Thyrza a photograph of the house up the Yang-tse-Kiang in which Mark and he lived in China.

"What a large house, monsieur!"

"Yes, we found our diggings too big for us, so we divided the one great room into several little ones.   Not half bad, was it?"

"I have the pagoda one too, Jack."

"So I see.   It's a capital photograph.   There is a temple right at the top of the rock, mademoiselle, most beautifully ornamented with carvings.   A flight of a thousand steps leads up to it, cut out in the solid stone, and it is a ticklish affair to climb up as the rock is pretty nearly perpendicular, and the river, which is very deep at that point, flows below.   Are there many foxes about here, Mr. Lefroy?"

"Abundance and to spare.   I am not a hunting man myself, and I prefer pheasants to foxes.   Sometimes the keeper shoots a fox by mistake."

"This must be a stiff country to ride over with the hills, but there are no hedges and comparatively few ditches."

"Not many hunt; so few can afford the time

and the money for the horses. But there is a subscription pack of hounds, and if you like to subscribe the Master will be very glad to gain another member."

" Not worth while for all the time I shall be at Carmylie. I had nearly forgotten Charity's message. It is about mademoiselle's coming to Carmylie. Will you all come to-morrow to afternoon tea and croquet?"

"I don't think we have any engagement," says Miss Lefroy. " So we shall be delighted to accept her invitation; unless, indeed, the day should be hopelessly wet."

" That is a thing which we can never depend upon. Why does not some one invent an apparatus for making sunshine and fine weather to order? It is one beauty of living in the tropics, you can count on a long tract of fine weather right ahead," replies Jack.

" I hope it wont rain. To arrange an open-air party, and then for the rain to appear to spoil it all is so very annoying and disheartening."

" Well, Miss Lefroy, as I wish to get back in time for dinner, I must be moving."

" Wont you dine with us?" she asks.

" Thanks very much, but not to-night. Good-bye, mademoiselle, you will see to-morrow what a wild place your lines are cast in for the future."

" If you wont be induced to remain, Jack, I'll come part of the way with you."

" All right, Luke."

And the two men walk off, both smoking like chimneys. " Blessed be the man who invented sleep," said Sancho Panza, Don Quixote's amusing follower. And blessed, thrice blessed be the memory of Sir Walter Raleigh who introduced the use of the soothing weed, echo the votaries of nicotine. The man who smoketh not is to be pitied. He may, it is true, save some few shillings but he loses more than he gains. The non-smoker can form no conception of the delicious moments of contemplation—the pleasant reveries—the untold bliss contained in a " *Tip cat*"—the enchantment which spreads out with the grey vapour—the clever ideas and happy thoughts which flash across the brain, while the smoker, contented and at peace with all the world, puffs out clouds under the influence of Raleigh's tranquillizing discovery. And if the *man* is to be pitied, how *much* more that man's *wife !* No pipe of peace to be smoked in which the domestic troubles and vexations, all aggravations and that odious " little bill " (still unpaid), vanish away with the fumes of the tobacco, and irate Benedict returns with the house of his mind swept and garnished from the evil spirit, even ready to indulge his offending spouse with a new bonnet or to look with favourable eyes on Worth's last account for that duck of a gown.

"Snug box that, Luke," says Jack, looking back at Lillieshill, lying in the afternoon sun among the green lace-like leaves of its beech woods. "I suppose it will be yours some time or other. What a lucky fellow you are!"

"Why, yes; unless Uncle Richard should marry."

"Jove! you don't think he will?"

"Well, one can never be certain of those old boys. They often end by marrying girls of eighteen. You don't catch them taking any much older. They think women are not like wine, and don't improve by keeping. But I should imagine he would not. It would break Aunt Fanny's heart, and no other woman would let him fiddle about the housekeeping as she does."

"Luke, what becomes of fellows who are bankrupts? One continually sees in the list of sequestrations, so-and-so is smashed, and there is the finis."

"Don't know, I am sure. Oh, they must of course get something to do. But that reminds me—are you going to keep Carmylie on your hands and settle there, or let it and go out to China again?"

" That depends upon circumstances. To begin with, Carmylie must be sold at once. There is no question about that. It seems my father had not long bought it before the bank in which most of his money was placed collapsed, and he sold part of the moors and mortgaged the rest; so the creditors come upon it."

"Whew!" says Mark. "What was the mortgage for?"

" £45,000. That is covered by the property. But my father must have been infatuated, for instead of resting content and living quietly, he went in for horses and jockeys and trainers. There are heaps of debt, but I have only been at home a couple of days, and have not had time to give more than a cursory glance at his papers, and cannot tell yet what the sum total will be."

" My dear fellow, it's a pretty go."

" Yes, that it just is! I should not care a hang, but there is my mother, who has been accustomed to nothing but luxury all her life. I am going to offer the creditors what I had laid by, towards a composition, and I think I shall sell my share of the business in Shanghai, and buy a partnership in England, that is, if I can get anything worth having, for every profession seems overstocked. Then I should take a comfortable villa near the town where my business was situated for the old lady, and the creditors would, perhaps, come to terms. I would pay so much a year, and clear off interest and principal at the same time."

" I would not sell the business in Shanghai, Jack. It's ten to one you get anything so good in England."

" Well, there's sense in that, Luke. But it is for the sake of my mother. She depends entirely upon me, and does not want me to go abroad again, as she thinks she will never see me again. And of course it is on the cards she may not. Anyway, I shall insure in her favour, so that if I go first she will be all serene."

" Your father never treated you kindly, Jack."

" Oh, well, he's gone now."

" Dead or alive, that doesn't matter, he did not treat you well. People should have more consideration for those who come after them than to leave everything in a muddle. He never spent a penny more on you than he could help. As for William, he lavished hundreds on him."

" William deserved that he should."

" You did not know of this in Shanghai ?"

" No, I had not the vestige of an idea of it ; I thought I was coming home, like the prodigal, to a snug competency. As far as I can make out there is a good deal of money invested in foreign railway shares, and some in mining companies, which last have gone to grief since I came back."

" It's a bad look-out. Do you think you will ever get clear ?"

" 'Pon my word, it's impossible to say. When I have found out the extent of the liabilities I shall be better able to judge. I think the governor must have been taken in by the lawyers. You never saw such accounts as they have sent in, pages long. I shall go to Edinburgh next month to see the solicitors. Carmylie is to be advertised immediately for sale, and we shall have to turn out next February."

" Disagreeable time of year to move, too."

" I do not see how it can be managed sooner."

" This will keep you a poor man, Jack. What a pity it is, and you were getting on so well ! If I could ——"

" Thanks, old fellow. I know what you mean. But I could not, and it would be of no use. You'll hear of me turning up as a billiard-marker at the other end of the world some of these days; or, Luke, make me your coachman. I'll close with you for a hundred per annum. I've often thought a gentleman's coachman has a good time of it."

" Well, Jack, if it should come worse——"

" I shall know where to come to, shan't I ? But I shan't all the same. I never was the chap to whom money took kindly. It was you who were born with a silver spoon in your mouth. Don't you remember in the old school-days at the Blue Coat, that when we were both tipped, your sovereign always lasted till nearly the end of the half, but mine had always been spent when we had been about a month at school, and I never could tell how it went for the life of me !"

" I say, Jack," says Mark, reflectively.

" Well !"

" Have you no convenient old party belonging to you whom you could persuade would be happier in a better sphere than this ?"

" And leave me all his or her tin ?"

" Yes."

" We had one, and a lot of good it has done us. But he was the only one of the species. And if there was another, you may be sure he would not die when wanted, but stick on like old boots, just out of sheer perversity. Those

old duffers never die, but live out those who are
waiting for their shoes. That field looks as if it
ought to be a good cover for partridges. I
should like to have a day's shooting here in the
autumn."

CHAPTER VIII.

MRS. FERRIER, with Charity, Jack, and Mrs. Napier's children, Rosie and David, are seated at lunch in the dining-room of Carmylie.

Time has dealt very leniently with Alice Ferrier, and her still luxuriant black hair is but little streaked with grey. Never exactly beautiful, she is not much faded or withered. She is one of those women who, without possessing any special brilliant or dazzling qualities of mind or body, are almost as pleasing when advanced in life as when in their earliest youth. These women always look nice and seem younger than their real age. Their dresses invariably suit them; their skirts never fall down in the mud when they think they have fastened them up safely; their dispositions are not angular nor filled with "wills and wonts;" they do not take desponding views of things in general; and surest and truest test of all, their relations love them, and their husbands and children worship them. Not particularly clever and with only a fair share of good looks, Mrs. Ferrier had won all hearts during her residence at Carmylie. Her own sex called her " Dear Mrs. Ferrier," and the opposite named her " Ferrier's pleasant wife." To her the loss of husband and son at one tremendous blow was an affliction so great that it was weeks before she could bring herself to mention the names of either again. Added to this was the sudden and unexpected change from opulence to the calculation of how far every shilling could be made to go.

The dining-room at Carmylie is not a very cheerful looking apartment, the walls being painted a dull mud colour, and the arms of the Campbells—who formerly owned the estate— emblazoned over the mantelpiece is the one attempt in the ornamental line.

The house itself is a grey, bleak building situated at the top of precipitous cliffs over-hanging the sea, here called the Bay of Car-mylie. Behind lies a small valley and the Glencairn mountains. Neither ivy nor creep-ing plants of any description are trained over the bare walls. Carmylie stands dreary and solitary, straight and severe, giving a much greater sense of desolation than the wild, barren hills which guard it on the one side, or the long lines of sterile cliffs, in a cleft of which is perched the fishing village, which wall the coast, on the other.

Houses after a time show tokens of the owner's character, and Carmylie looks as if it had a history. And so indeed it has. The grim old place has changed hands often. In the tunnel on which its foundations are laid, many a Jacobite has hidden when a price was set on his head; and a little later on, many a smuggler has stolen up the secret staircase leading from the kitchen region to the vast dark attics that extend over the top storey, and hidden there the casks of whisky above-proof, and bales of French silks, and boxes of cigars, for which no duty had been paid. Many are those who have breathed their last, and been carried forth through the shade-haunted corridors to the kirk-yard down the brae at the fishing village beside the sea, and many the happy brides who have driven off from the narrow bolt upright door amidst a shower of satin slippers and wedding-cake. Like all Scotch country houses, it has its ghosts, derived probably from floating local traditions of events which happened so long ago that it is impossible to separate fact from fancy.

The windows of Carmylie are small and not very numerous. At the time of erection the modern ideas on the subject of ventilation were still a hundred years in the future, and the window-tax pressing heavily on the purses of the lieges, our ancestors ruthlessly sacrificed the advantages of l'ght and fresh air to economy. A few straggling larches grow close to the house. The gravel sweep up to the front door is ill kept and covered with weeds, the lawn does not seem to have been mown for months; the only sign of the place being inhabited is a row of bee-hives among some flower-beds, which give evidence of receiving more attention than the other parts of the grounds. It is not an inviting house to fix upon as a permanent dwelling. During the summer months, as now, while the sun shines and the weather is fine, the prospect of passing some time there does not appear so unendurable; but one shudders to think of it as a home on a dull day in November, when the mist settles on the hill tops and lies curled in the deep mountain gorges; or on a cold, frosty night when the wind whistles down from the broad shoulder of the Witch's Law, cutting like a knife, moaning and sighing like a poor lost spirit through the thin larch boughs to the sea, over the great sand bar where so many good ships have struck and stranded, going to the bottom with all hands and not a soul left to tell the tale.

Then one would naturally wish for the bustle and noise of a town, with the gaslights, the sounds of the cabs and carriages, and the tokens of life and business and amusement, from all of which Carmylie is as isolated as though built in the middle of the Sahara.

Yet Carmylie is not without a certain wild, stern beauty of its own. To be sure, it has no smooth, smiling meadows, no purling streams of which to boast; but those who love the sweep of a bold, rocky coast, the spread of brown moors, the green mantle and aromatic spice of pine woods, the golden bloom of whins and broom, and the purple of heather, the wide expanse of water, would find much in which to delight at Carmylie. The air from the mountains is pure, bracing and magnificently clear, and an artist would be able to fill scores of canvasses with the effects of light and shade on glen, wood, and sea, while the red-and-white fishing village, with its natural pier of rocks, its winding street, its kirk and kirk-yard, would in themselves furnish subjects for many sketches. Ferrier has justly described Carmylie when he said, that besides the fisher-folks and the minister there is no society. So it may readily be supposed that Charity

Napier, accustomed to the gaiety which attends an Indian station containing five regiments, who were among the fastest in the army, should complain of being buried alive.

The Carmylie estate was originally of large extent, but is now reduced to a few small farms, the house and grounds, and some moors for shooting. These are all that remain of the former broad lands. For this the Campbells themselves were partly to blame, and disastrous '45, which ruined so many families in Scotland, bringing her noblest and best to the block, had also a great deal for which to answer. The Campbells were an extravagant race and seemed born with a fatal facility for spending money. While gifted with beauty of person and amiability of disposition, they were also endowed with an awkward and uncomfortable habit of being unable to refuse acquiescence when events required a decided negative, or to deny themselves anything which appeared to them desirable to possess.

The immediate consequence of this want of backbone or moral strength, was that Carmylie was put up for sale.

Luck undoubtedly runs in families and seems to be attached to certain houses. In this respect Carmylie appeared possessed by an avenging

Greek fate. Mr. Ferrier had been a prosperous man, content to live quietly on his small property at Blackbeck House in Lincolnshire, until a relative died, leaving him a large fortune, on which he purchased Carmylie, and from that moment began going the pace which kills. This pace, however agreeable, cannot be long kept up, and the rate at which Mr. Ferrier went was so mad and furious that the only wonder was he did not go to smash sooner. But business men know that occasionally immense sums of money may be made without money. Mr. Ferrier had some knowledge of this method, and before involving himself in the troubles and expenses of lawyers' mortgages, made sundry efforts to redeem himself by " flying paper." Unfortunately, he was unsuccessful. He never tried to reduce his expenditure and kept up two establishments all the year round, one at Melton Mowbray, and the other at Carmylie. There never had been such gay times known in the county as when Mr. Ferrier came down to Carmylie for the shooting season. There was open house from the 12th of August until December 10th ; Champagne flowed like water at never less than twelve shillings a bottle, balls, dances, fêtes, dinners.

Then, first one moor was parted with and then another. The property was mortgaged to the last halfpenny of its value, and for several years before his death Mr. Ferrier lived not only up to his income, but very much beyond it.

The sudden illness and death of his eldest son, William, a promising young man, in whom all his hopes were centred, was a great shock to his system, from which he never rallied, and he died, leaving his wife totally unprovided for. His lawyers considered it a merciful removal, as he was spared the pain of being obliged to declare himself bankrupt, and at his advanced age it would have been impossible for him to begin anew in any profession.

So Jack was summoned home from China by Mrs. Ferrier. At that time she had no idea to what an extent her husband's affairs were involved, and it was not until Jack's arrival at Carmylie that he was informed of his father's debts, which to clear off will be the work of years.

The first step towards economizing had been made as soon as Mrs. Ferrier's lawyers acquainted her with the state of things, and Mr. Ferrier's fine stud was sold by the instructions of the solicitors, along with the house at Melton Mowbray, and the household at Carmylie reduced to the lowest scale compatible with comfort and ordinary respectability. Charity was well off being liberally supplied with money by Captain Napier.

"The governess comes to-day," says Mrs. Napier. "I don't imagine she is very proficient in her profession, but she will do until we leave Carmylie, and I got her cheap. She is Mr. Mark's protégée."

"What is the damage, Charity?" asks Ferrier.

"Not very deadly, twenty pounds a year."

"As much as you pay your maid! It is too little. What is she to do?"

"Undertake the entire charge of the children and their wardrobes, as the advertisements say."

"Oh, poor little girl, you can't expect her to manage with that. I'll give you a ten pound note towards making it thirty."

"It is horrible to be so poor," pursues Mrs. Napier; "Carmylie was so different in poor dear papa's time," raising her lace-edged handkerchief to her eyes. "There was plenty of society and lots going on."

"As Clough says, 'How lucky it is to have money, heigh ho! How lucky it is to have money!' The fellow who wrote the other day some nonsense about virtue and rubies, had never known what it is to be without sixpence in the world."

" It is odd Miss Rutherfurd's people should live at Marshley," says Mrs. Ferrier. " What is she like ?"

" Tall, scraggy, red nose, uncertain temper, and of an awkward age. By-the-bye, mother, what is an awkward age? Jack, I have asked the Lefroys and MacNabs to-day."

" I wish you would not, Charity."

" It is not so expensive as a dinner to have them to afternoon tea, and you can't expect to be asked out, unless you give something in return. I asked the MacNabs on your account."

" On *my* account ?"

" Yes, for you. We have plenty of blue blood, and pedigrees and so on. What we want is a little hard cash in the family. You see I am married already."

" Otherwise you would be willing to sacrifice yourself for the good of the family. Then I am glad your fate is sealed."

" But the MacNabs are nice lady-like girls."

" And I fear they may remain so for me. If matters are only going to get straight by marrying some one with money, they will not be set right by me. I shan't present you with a sister-in-law."

"I am not sorry, Jack; they are generally great nuisances."

"There's Rattray with the letters," announces Rosie, running to open the door.

"Weel, laird, we hae gotten gude weather at last," says a voice in broad Scotch, belonging to a short thickset man, with merry twinkling eyes, grey hair, and cheeks ruddy like a ripe American apple. He is Ferrier's factotum for three days during the week; on the alternate three, he is the walking post between Carmylie and the post town of Queensmuir. "I hae broucht the tabaky," continues Rattray, tranquilly, "it's the best tae be got in Queensmuir, but I'm some doubting it's no extra gude, and I hae paid the tailor, and here's the receipt, and gotten your fishing-breeks wi' me, and Rosie's new bonnet, and it's tae be houpit Mrs. Napier will be pleased *this* time."

Whereupon Rattray delivers the postbag to Ferrier, and a bandbox tied up in a red pocket-handchief to Charity, but so far from leaving the room on having fulfilled his duty, he remains while Charity tries on Rosie's hat, to judge of the effect.

Rosie is a pretty child with a fresh fair complexion, blue eyes, and yellow hair, which she wears cut over her forehead, in exactly the same way as her mother's. Her brother Davie is another edition of herself, with shorter hair, dressed in knickerbockers. The pair are twins, of the age of eight or nine years, and as full of mischief and impudence as two spoiled children can be.

"Any news from Queensmuir, Rattray, or the village?" asks Ferrier, who enjoys a talk with that worthy.

"No just onything in parteeklar," returns Rattray, unwilling to commit himself so far as to say there is any news, but on the other hand anxious to keep up his reputation for hearing the *on dits* of the burgh before any one else. "There's an auld wife near killed wi' furious driving by the lad Nicol, the young doctor, ye ken ; and I *did* hear that our minister, Mr. Dods, is to tak' a wife."

"Poor man ! I am sorry for him," says Ferrier.

"Fat for ? Taking a wife ? Weel, there is nae dout but that whiles it is a sairious trial till a man. But I'm thinking Miss Jean Cockburn will not be to hae him. He has no eneuch o' money. And ye ken women wad marry auld Nick gin he wad keep them aye braw."

"And very right of them too," laughs Ferrier. "Rosie, open the sideboard and you will find some whisky in a bottle; pour out Rattray a glass."

"Thank ye kindly," says Rattray, holding up the "mountain dew" between himself and the light with an appreciative glance. "And here's your gude health, laird, and the mistress yonder, and Mrs. Napier, and Davie, and Rosie's. I daursay it wadna be the waur o' a drappie watter."

"You need not put in any water, Rattray," exclaims truthful Rosie, hastily, "for mamma put in *plenty* yesterday, when Uncle Jack was at Lillieshill."

"That's right, Rosie," returns Jack, "speak the truth and shame old Scratch. Rattray, give me your glass, and I'll pour a little more whisky in."

"Has Cecilia been writing any more poetry, Rattray? What did you think of her last piece?" inquires Mrs. Ferrier.

Rattray's eyes twinkle. He pauses before he answers, and then makes response—

"Tae speak the truth and tell no lees, *no muckle ava !* But I was up Bogg water yestreen, and I catched four dizzen o' trout, and I can tell ye I think vera muckle o' *them.* Na, na. It's no for women folks to write bits o' poetry. *That's* no their business. Besides, women's poetry is nae better than a curren' rubbishin' havers !"

"You are a very ungallant man! If I were Cecilia, I should be most indignant," laughs Mrs. Napier.

"Ah !" very prolonged, "Cecilia kens better than that."

"What are you going to do with that dreadful instrument of torture, Rattray ?" asks Ferrier. Rattray has an ancient blunderbuss in his hand—a weapon of great age, deeply valued and admired by him. Friends and acquaintances, however, are apt to keep at a respectful distance when they perceive him coming near with his formidable gun.

"Shoot the spuggies," he answers.

"I wont allow you to shoot the dear little sparrows; they are my particular friends," says Rosie.

"Weel, Rosie, I am real sorry to hear you say that," he calmly replies; "I had nae notion they could be friends o' *yours*, for they are just the *blaggairds* o' the feathered creation. Did ye think I sow paes and neeps for thae rapscallions to tak' the heads off? I'm gaein' oot the noo till hae a shot at them."

"I am coming too' says Davie.

Rattray sprinkles treacherously handfuls of oatmeal on the ground.

"Mind yersel noo," he calls out, "I am just aboot till fire."

"Let me pull the trigger," shouts Davie. An awful explosion is heard. One sparrow lies prone and hors-de-combat on the earth. Rattray picks it up, and caresses affectionately the mass of fluffy feathers.

Cecilia, the wife of his bosom, pops her head out of the kitchen window, and shrieks loudly.

"Nae harm's dune," says Rattray, confidentially. "Sae ye needna skirl!"

"What a mercy the governess is coming, Rosie and Davie are really quite unmanageable!" exclaims Mrs. Napier. "They have been so much with Rattray, that they have begun to speak quite broad Scotch, and when children begin to speak badly it is so difficult to break them of it."

"They certainly seem to have been allowed to run wild," remarks Jack.

"Oh yes; but who could think of anything with poor dear papa, and dear Willie. and my own health too being so weak. I sometimes think, Jack, that you do not feel their loss much."

"I am as down in the mouth about it as anyone can be; but there is no use in letting people see it," he returns. "You would not have me sit down and cry like a girl who has lost her lover, instead of putting one's shoulder to the wheel, Charity?"

"I am sure Rattray is smoking in the kitchen. I should not allow him to do that," rejoins Mrs. Napier. "It is for you to speak. You are the master."

"Oh, let him have his whiff!"

"Oh, well. I suppose you must do as you like about it. And, Jack, don't be out of the way when the MacNabs come."

"You wont want me to play croquet?"

"No, not for your own pleasure; but it always makes girls better tempered when there is an unmarried nice-looking eligible in the place."

"A nice eligible I am to be sure," says Ferrier, laughing.

"Well, and you were my pet brother, Jack. Really that tobacco! It is poisonous! Do tell Rattray at least to shut the kitchen door."

Rattray is sitting on the kitchen dresser with his legs dangling like Mahomet's coffin, between heaven and earth, and his fingers fumble restlessly in his pockets; which symptom, by long

experience, his wife is aware means he is searching for his pipe. In a few moments he fills the
room and passages with the perfumes of the
very vilest and stalest *pigtail* to be bought at
Carmylie village.

He hears the sound of approaching footsteps
and departs hastily, and when Ferrier appears
to reprimand him he has fled, and is slowly
sauntering through the walks in the vegetable
garden, pronouncing judgment on the peas and
reflecting whether he will " stick " the late row,
or make a new scarecrow to terrify the thieving
blackbirds, against whom he wages malignant
war, while Cecilia solemnly asseverates on being
called to account for her husband's misde-
meanors—

" As sure as *daith*, she disna ken wha was
smoking. It will just be the *peat-reek*, sir."

Ferrier shuts himself up in his study to look
over the factor's books, and write a letter to his
partner, Esmé Lennox ; but has not long settled
himself when he is summoned by Rosie to play
croquet with the MacNabs and the Lillieshill
people.

In other days there was a flower garden
where the croquet lawn is now situated ; but the
beds have long since departed, leaving no traces of
their former gay denizens beyond a star of snow-

drops which appears in spring regularly as the new year comes round. A low moss-covered wall runs between the green and the orchard, a wilderness of a place with ground ivy and periwinkles growing in profusion over the earth among the old fruit trees.

Thyrza feels a different creature since her visit to Lillieshill, more self-reliant, less nervous. The lazy, easy country life has opened out a wider world to her than that of the narrow circumscribed horizon of the Villios *pension*. A very little makes her happy and bright—a very little, a passing look, a changed tone of voice is sufficient to render her sad; a smile, a kind word are so much to her. The knowledge of being well and becomingly dressed, added to the consciousness that she is about to become a real, and independent worker, and to be of some use in the world, gives her a sensation of importance entirely new to her.

Her luggage has never turned up again, so Miss Lefroy has bought her some inexpensive summer dresses, and presented her with a black silk, made with a square cut body for an evening, and Thyrza has expressly stipulated to be allowed to repay her when she receives her first quarter's salary. She wears a dust coloured print, a knot of scarlet ribbon at her throat, a black fichu, and a black hat of rather a coquettish shape, which suits the brown face and its dark hair.

Ferrier introduces Thyrza thus—

" Mother, this is mademoiselle."

Mrs. Ferrier does not shake hands coldly as if greeting a stranger, but welcomes the girl with a warm kiss, which renders Thyrza her devoted admirer for life.

" These are your pupils, Miss Rutherfurd," says Mrs. Napier, bringing the twins forward.

" My name is Mischief," volunteers Rosie ; " Uncle Jack gave me it because I let the pigs out one day and chased them round the garden."

" And what is your name ? " she asks of David, who is peering curiously at his future preceptress.

" Come and shake hands directly with mademoiselle," commands Ferrier.

" I don't want to see the new governess," protests Davie, sulkily.

" Oh, Monsieur David," cries Thyrza, pronouncing the word with the *a broad*, as in the French language.

" She's speaking *Scotch ;* how *vulgar !*" exclaims Rosie, laughing loudly.

" Shut up, you little beggars !" storms Ferrier, with a frown.

Thyrza may be good for nothing. Most likely

she is.　She confesses to a predilection for *fast* things.　She may combine all the most disagreeable qualities of his detested and abhorred fashionable woman, but as long as she is in his house she is to be treated with respect.

"That is not the way to behave to mademoiselle," he continues.

Mrs. Napier observes Jack's interference in Thyrza's behalf with displeasure.　She hopes he is not going to make an idiot of himself about *that* girl.　He ought to know better.　Unless he marries money he cannot marry at all.　Besides, she is such an exceedingly plain, wild looking girl, and so dark, as black as a crow or a gipsy.　But men are great noodles and will sometimes rave about people whom Charity can see nothing in, either to like or admire.　There is Lola MacNab, with her fortune, ready to hand, just as if specially created by Providence on purpose for Jack.　She does not believe what he says with regard to disliking the idea of being tied to any woman without the chance of changing his mind.　Cecil Napier said the same thing, and within two months of making the remark was engaged to Charity.

"Will you have me as a partner, mademoiselle?" goes on Ferrier.　"I don't pretend to know much of the game, but I will do what I can."

"Oh, that will *never* do, Jack," interrupts Charity, hastily. "Two inexperienced players should not be on the same side. Miss MacNab and you will be a much better arrangement."

"With the greatest pleasure," answers Ferrier, readily. "A crack player such as I understand Miss MacNab to be, will be a vast assistance to mademoiselle and myself."

"The very first time I took a mallet in my hand I went the round of the green without stopping. I am a first rate hand at all games, particularly so."

"I dare say, Mr. Lefroy; beginners at billiards often make better scores at first than professionals, but it does not last. It is luck, not skill, and, of course, in the long run, real play must tell."

"What are the sides to be?" asks Mark, swinging his mallet round and round, and then hitting several balls one after another in a vague undecided way.

"Eight is such a stupid game. There is time to go for a constitutional between the turns," says Mrs. Napier.

"How would this do? Mr. Lefroy; you, Charity; Miss MacNab and Mr. Dods : then the others, Mademoiselle, Miss Jane, Mark, and I. Shall we toss up, Mark, heads or tails?"

"Tails," rejoins Mark. "Tails always do turn up, don't they?"

"I thought Miss MacNab was going to play with you, Jack."

"Oh, I am sure I apologize, Miss MacNab. I merely thought you would find Mr. Lefroy a better partner than myself."

"I am quite content with the other arrangement," says Lola, a little piqued at being thrown over rather unceremoniously to the lot of the older man.

"I vote we *all* play," remarks Mr. Dods, in his solemn slow voice. "We can divide into sets of four. I have seen two games played at once on the same green; the two sets starting from opposite posts."

"So have I, Mr. Dods, but it was very tiresome. One had continually to stop in the middle of a shot to pick up a ball or wait until the other set had played out a turn," objects Jane MacNab, energetically. "We always met midway."

Finally it is settled to play a game of eight.

The minister begins operations.

In his long black coat and white choker he looks grave enough to justify Lola MacNab's assertion that he surely has lately been conducting a funeral service. He expresses himself in a peculiarly leisurely voice, with pauses between each sentence. He is a person to whom, no matter how free and easy he has been with you on the previous evening, you always seem to require a fresh introduction on your next meeting.

But Mr. Dods, in spite of his ceremonious, pompous manners, knows good wine when he tastes it; he is also a judge of a pretty girl, and a general admirer of the sex. He is the best relator of an anecdote in the neighbourhood, telling the most absurd incidents without moving a muscle of his countenance, while his auditors are convulsed with laughter. After a few glasses of port, or a stiff tumbler of toddy, when fairly roused and set a-going, Mr. Dods is a pleasant enough companion, more especially as he does not intrude his religious opinions upon those of a different communion, and whatever he may *preach*, certainly does not *practise* sour Calvinistic views.

On account of these qualities, and having in common with Mr. Lefroy an excellent opinion of himself—after all, the world generally takes one at one's own estimate—" so long as thou doest well unto thyself men will speak good of thee" Mr. Dods has many friends, and whenever there is a dinner-party on the *tapis* within twenty miles of the manse of Carmylie, is in

request for the " pleasure of his company."
Besides, Mr. Dods is not a married man, and is
an object of considerable interest to various
maiden ladies in the vicinity, none of whom
would have had any objection to reside at
Carmylie Manse, which they understand is
already well stocked with linen and furniture,
having been Mr. Dods' father's before him, so
there could be little difficulty about settling
down.

Unfortunately for the aspirations of the
spinsters, Mr. Dods prefers wandering about the
country instead of " settling like a reasonable
man," and attending to the duties of his parish ;
he generally starts the first thing on Monday
morning, and returns at the eleventh hour on
Saturday night ; indeed, on several occasions,
he has never put in an appearance at all on
the Sabbath at the kirk, the congregation waiting patiently for him, and only going home
when the precentor announced it was useless
remaining longer, the minister doubtless having
missed the train, or met with some accident.

In anyone else this conduct would have been
visited with disapproval and a hint of the
Presbytery, but Mr. Dods is a privileged
man, and no one hauls *him* over the coals. His
lady friends hold steadfastly to their faith that

if he were only married and had a wife to look
after him people would see the difference in his
behaviour *then*.   Mr. Dods thinks so too, but
with a trifling alteration.   In the summer he
usually has a number of visitors, chiefly ladies,
at the Manse, having a married lady to act as
chaperone.   Dull in the Manse ! He is never
there long enough at a time to experience
weariness.

Jane MacNab means playing the game, the
whole game, and nothing but the game.   With
her it is not a pleasure to while away the
passing moment, but an absorbing business.
She flies from one end of the green to the
other ; routs out Mr. Lefroy whenever Lola and
he are trying to "*spoon;*" rushes up and down "to
give a line ;" attacks players who are chattering
instead of taking a lively interest in the game,
and decides disputed points, such as if a ball
may be considered fairly through its hoop when
half way—and is indefatigable beyond all praise.

" No doubt, Mr. Mark, you will find a great
difference between the society here and that in
Shanghai," observes Mr. Dods.

" No, I can't say I do. We went out to dinner
there, or spent the evening at a friend's house,
picked them and the grub to pieces afterwards,
and abused them *well*. Then met them next day,

and said how much we had enjoyed ourselves as politely as possible, just as we do here."

" That does not speak well for society, Mr. Mark."

" But society cannot exist without an amount of shams. How terrible it would be if every-one spoke his mind and the exact truth. It would end in everyone fighting and killing every-body until none was left, after the fashion of the celebrated Kilkenny cats. Imagine paying a call, and being greeted with, ' My dear fellow, I wish you far enough, but as you *are* here, &c. &c.' I've often said how delighted I was, and so on, when I've internally been awfully bored."

" But is not that untruthful ?"

" Well, I suppose it is. It's a choice between saying what you don't exactly mean, and hurting a person's feelings. The fact is, politeness is very often a test of self-denial. I think I would sooner tell a white lie——"

" If there *are* white lies," says Ferrier.

" Than wound a sensitive man who may, per-haps, brood over your stray remark, and make himself miserable for days. If one is to live and let live, one must humour people's foibles a little."

" Even at the expense of truth ?"

" I don't see why one could not combine civility and truth," replies the minister.

" It's a more difficult matter than you might suppose. I show you a picture of my own painting, Mr. Dods. You cannot, in accordance with your conscience, call it anything but frightfully ugly, but I shall be intensely mortified if you do not admire it.   Well !"

" Ah, we-el."

" Now, Mr. Dods."

" Excuse me, Mr. Lefroy," says Jane MacNab, " but I fancy I saw you move your ball into position."

" Ah, eh, oh !" exclaims Mr. Lefroy, caught in the very act of kicking his ball in *front* of his hoop, " I thought it was my turn."

"We-el," rejoins Mr. Dods, " I sincerely hope I may never be so situated, Mr. Mark."

" You don't call that an answer, do you, Mr. Dods ?" laughs Mark.

" I don't much like those very strictly truthful people, Mr. Dods. I hope you are not shocked ! But they resemble a certain class of extremely pious persons," observes Charity, " who are always treading on your toes and making disagreeable remarks (generally true, too), without the least consideration for your feelings."

> " Oh, wad the power the giftie gie us,
>   To see ourselves as ithers see us,"

quotes Mr. Dods.

" Heaven forbid," says Ferrier, pausing to hit the stick. " It would be a most objectionable present. What is wanted is a process by which our neighbours shall see *us* as *we* see ourselves. Then the world would be as full of living perfection as, judging from the epitaphs on tombstones, it is of departed saints."

" Look at the enemy; they are flourishing like the green bay-tree of the wicked, but you will see it wont last. It is your turn now, Mr. Lefroy. This is your hoop. You go through; hit Miss MacNab; croquet her down to me with the following stroke, ' take two off ' from Jack, and away to your next hoop, and then——"

Mr. Lefroy prepares to make his stroke. Mark goes down on his knees to see that his mallet is all right.

" A little further in; no—to yourself. That's it. You have changed it again. There, now you *must* come through without fail."

" They'll get it right sooner or later," remarks Ferrier to Thyrza.

" Just a thought more to yourself," counsels Mark. Mr. Lefroy obediently moves the position and is arranged according to Mark's ideas, when the loud report of a gun is heard in the orchard close by, followed by a louder exclamation. Mr. Lefroy gives a start, hits his ball with the side of his mallet, and the result is an unmitigated miss.

"The mallet twisted," says Mr. Lefroy, looking rather foolish at this ending to all the elaborate preparations, "and I really believe it is a crooked one. I cannot play well with a crooked mallet."

"Any person killed?" asks Ferrier, looking over the wall into the orchard; "it is Rattray with the blunderbuss, I am always afraid of some accident happening with it."

"Mr. Dods, *do* come up," implores Mrs. Napier. This is exactly what the minister has vainly attempted to do through the whole game, so it is hardly to be expected he will succeed now.

Croquet has been rendered so extremely scientific lately, that a good deal of the pleasure formerly attending this pleasant mode of spending a few hours in the open air is departed. But besides being scientific, it can also be made a very irritating game. If spitefully inclined, a skilful player can bully or worry his opposing enemy to death while really remaining within bounds, and in no way exceeding the rules and regulations. As at other games, the old fable of the hare and the tortoise is often verified at croquet. The last is not seldom first. The gay free lance, who wanders over the green, striking terror into the hearts of sober stayers at their hoops is frequently left behind at the close, while the slow coaches who have plodded from ring to ring with patient perseverance win the game easily, proving the truth of the adage, " Slow and sure wins the race."

Most people get a little hot over croquet. Even the meekest of maidens, whom no one suspects of possessing any temper at all, grave church dignitaries, learned barristers and professors, and worthy ministers like Mr. Dods will dispute violently, and argue to the last gasp over some trifling point of play. For it is not in human nature to be taken from a delightful position in front of your hoop, made use of in helping your enemy through *his* rings, or in waging war against your own side, and finally be sent adrift, without experiencing a slight conviction it would afford you a pleasing sensation to do likewise to *that* ball which has put you to the rout, and scattered you and your companions to the four corners of the globe.

" Tired, mademoiselle ?" asks Ferrier.

" No, monsieur."

" Then what are you sighing for ? Because you have the bad luck to be a girl ? Misfortune to which you will have to submit, as it cannot be altered. You would never have done for a man, unless you had got a new set of dispositions, feelings, and character."

"Why not?" says Thyrza, making a dashing long shot from one stick to the other, and hitting the minister's ball, which evokes from him an astonished, "We—el! Miss Rutherfurd."

"Because—I will tell you afterwards. I know you are going to make a mull of this stroke. This is your last ring, is it not? If you play decently, the game is in your hands, and we shall win in a canter."

"It is all up, Mrs. Napier, I am afraid," remarks Mark. "Miss Thyrza has it all her own way. They will go out this time."

"Lola, will you oblige me by moving, I think there is a ball somewhere under your dress. Where is yours, Mr. Lefroy, I don't see it anywhere?"

"Oh, Jane, I am admiring the view; did you ever see anything so sweet as the sea, and the cliffs of St. Philip's to-day?"

Jane searches in vain for Mr. Lefroy's ball, and as it is in his coat-pocket in which he has hidden it until required, there is no wonder her labour is thrown away. Lola had not got much out of Mr. Lefroy in the way of "spooniness." It takes a good deal of wine to get him up to the mark, and while saying anything and every-thing, there is no fear of his committing him-self. Short of an offer in plain words he is perfectly safe. Soft looks, tender sentences; garnished with poetical quotations, count as nothing, and if she succeeds in leading Mr. Lefroy to "sacrifice" at the altar of Hymen, Lola will be a clever young woman. Thyrza sends Mr. Dods away, places herself in a good position, and having one stroke more tries the hoop, but becoming nervous, or her hand trem-bling at the critical moment, she blunders the little easy stroke as people so often do after executing something really difficult, and, striking the wire, her ball rebounds to the wrong side, without going through the ring.

"There! I was sure you would spoil it. You were in too great a hurry, and did not look to see if you were hitting straight. You would not have made me a good clerk in Shanghai."

"No! But I should only have had to add up accounts, and write *things* in a big book."

"That *is* clear and concise! I should some-times have wanted you to do other things be-sides writing in a big book."

"Going out shooting?"

"Not exactly. One time some of Mark's men and mine got into a row, and were put into prison, and he and I took a journey up country to speak to the mandarin of the town, where they were confined. We got separated, and I wandered over so many miles over the hills at night among the brushwood, a sort of prickly bush which grows there in great abundance, it tore my clothes to shreds, and scratched my face and legs until they were one mass of wounds. In this lively predicament, not knowing where I was, and not having the most remote notion how far distant the town was to which we were going, I tumbled up against something soft. There was a splendid moon shining, and by its light I saw that it was the body of a man with his throat cut in a horrible manner, nearly severing his head from his body. The Chinese, you know, never bring any dead body they find lying about, because if they did, the magistrates would consider them implicated in the death. Now, if you had been with me, you would have either fainted on the spot, or else had a fit from terror which would have rendered affairs more complicated for me."

"Monsieur is very——"

"Come, Mr. Ferrier, I do wish you would attend," interrupts Jane. "It is too bad! Everyone goes off and talks in the intervals between their turns, and they *never remember* where they are going, or when they ought to play."

"Oh, Miss Jane, that is too severe! I don't believe *you* ever hit the stick," says Mr. Lefroy, who has cheated shamefully, and only been through about half the hoops, so it is rather cool of him to complain of Jane MacNab. Jane, really vexed and angry, bestows an indignant look on her sister, upon whose ball she swoops down, and forthwith croquets to the inmost recess of a mazy hedge, whence it is rescued with infinite difficulty and trouble.

"You should have two greens, Mr. Ferrier," she remarks, resting on her mallet, and feeling considerably better after having wreaked her revenge on Lola, " one for people who do like to play, and another for those who merely mean to flirt and cheat."

"I am sure, Miss Jane," says the minister, deprecatingly, " I have been honourable, although once or twice sorely tempted, throughout."

"It was not you I meant," looking across at Mr. Lefroy.

He has deserted Lola and is paying attention to Mrs. Napier. In her half-mourning white dress and black sash, the former tucked up just enough to show her small feet in high-heeled shoes with diamond buckles, made after the fashion of the last century, she is a very agreeable figure for contemplation. Lola, even with her Parisian dresses, cannot attain the quiet elegance of Mrs. Napier, which is distracting alike to man and womankind.

" Mademoiselle, you are very pale, sit down. The seat is more comfortable than it looks. It is here I smoke my after-breakfast pipe ; but I generally bring a rug with me."

" Miss Jane, did you read the account in the *Scotsman* yesterday of the golf match at S. Philip's ?" asks Mr. Dods.

" Excuse me, I never talk at croquet," she returns, giving him the snub direct. " I like doing one thing well at a time, and prefer to watch the play."

" Monsieur was lost on the Chinese hills," says Thyrza. " Will you not finish ?"

" Well, I went on, and when daylight came found myself not very far from the town Chip-Cho-Hoang-Ho, where the mandarin lived. Wasn't I glad, that's all, to see some human beings again ? But I was such a spectacle what with mud and scratches, and not to mention the most part of my trousers being torn and destroyed, that some kind person spread a report I was a magician, and the entire population set on me with sticks and stones, and I had to bolt for my life."

" Did *you* run ?" inquires Thyrza, much interested.

" *Rather!* I showed them a clean pair of heels; for of course I was far out-matched and the odds were tremendous. I tore along to the mandarin's house, contriving to keep ahead of my pursuers. They were much fresher than I was, having had the advantage of their night's rest, while I had been on foot for hours. But the training I had had as a lad at " Hare and hounds" and " Paper chases" when at school served me now, and I dashed breathless into the hall of the mandarin's house. I was so winded I could not speak or perform the customary civilities, about which they are very particular. Luckily, Mark was there, and the presence of the mob, with my ragged, bleeding figure—I had got one or two nasty cuts from some stones the natives shied at me—sufficiently explained how things stood."

" I wish I had seen. you."

" I was hardly presentable for a lady's eyes, so it is fortunate you did not. The mandarin had the good sense to listen to reason ; he gave me a bath, and we procured some more decent clothing, and then we discussed the trade dispute. Our men were liberated; but the populace were so furious that the mandarin was obliged to grant us a guard of soldiers, between whom we marched out of Chip-Cho-Hoang-Ho, very glad to shake the dust of that city off our feet, and escorted into the country by the yells and execrations of the people."

" What did they say ?"

" Oh, little simple things such as ' Kill the English devils !' ' Slash them to bits,' and other cries of that kind. As they spoke Chinese, I understood all they said, and I could scarcely refrain from firing at them ; but I knew if I did nothing would prevent them from falling on us and tearing us to pieces ; and then our countrymen would have to put up a memorial to our memory, rejoicing that our loss had left an opening in the trade. It was no joke to keep cool when mud and missiles of divers sorts were whistling round our heads, and the men jeering and mocking and cursing us."

" It must have been splendid fun, and so exciting !" says Thyrza.

" I can't say I quite saw where the fun lay at the time," returns Ferrier, with a grim smile. " And you are welcome to that kind of excitement where I am concerned."

" Can you speak Chinese ?"

" Yes. It is next to impossible to get on with the natives unless you can acquire the language."

" Is it awfully difficult ?" asks Thyrza.

" It's not easy; worse than Greek; and you can't depend on interpreters—often frightful scamps."

" I wish now I had thought of going into business," says Mr. Dods; " the ministerial is not a money-making profession, and I think before long we ministers will have to strike, like the masons and mill-workers."

" China is not what it once was, and it is quite a mistake to think one has only to go out there and money comes of itself. A whole batch of poor young fellows threw up their appointments as clerks in London and came out to Shanghai," observes Mark. " They were nearly starved, and we had to get up a subscription for them to pay their passage home again. The fact is, that one requires interest and capital out at Shanghai as well as in England."

" Is the climate good ?"

" Not very; lots of yellow fever, and seven or eight out of every ten who take it on their arrival die. You would require to go out about twenty, or thereabouts, in order to get used to it. It is a good thing to get into the Chinese customs, if you can speak the language. Begin with a house at 50*l.* per month, which increases if you give satisfaction. In that case you can make plenty of money, and can trade on your own hook. If I was going to begin again I think I should try the Island of Formosa."

"Had I known what I do now, it would have been the very thing," answers Mr. Dods. "What do you think of the burgh of Queensmuir?"

"In much about the same condition as Shanghai was when I first knew it, as regards the streets. It has improved immensely of late years. I suppose you never heard the joke about Ferrier when he first arrived there. He had letters of introduction to the heads of a firm, and they, hearing of his landing, invited him to dine with them. So, after looking about the town a little he took up his abode in an hotel and donned his very best evening dress clothes. Of course he was anxious to cut a dash and make a good impression upon the gentlemen. So then he set off. It grows dark very suddenly in China, and the streets of Shanghai were neither paved nor lighted, and were very like a sea of mud, with lakes of water here and there.   A considerable gale was blowing, and somehow or another Ferrier tripped up, lost his balance, and fell headlong, all his length in the slush."

" What did he say ?" asks Mr. Dods.

" Something much too hot and strong to be repeated in your presence," says Ferrier, answering for himself. " I was in a holy frame of mind, more easily imagined than described, as novelists say when they come to an awkward bit.   I have often noticed that, after remarking, ' it is impossible to describe this scene,' they never fail to have a shy at it."

" And did you go to dinner ?"

" Hardly.   I went back to the hotel and sent an excuse to the people."

" Do you know Jack once made a plum-pudding ?   It was one Christmas, in Shanghai, Mrs. Napier.   It was a great big one, for fifty people, and was boiled in a cauldron. Jack had two fellows with long poles to stir it round."

" What, was it not boiled in a bag ?" exclaims Jane MacNab.

" Oh yes, it must have been, but still I recollect its being stirred round, and one of the men complaining of being too hot, Jack emptied a bucket of cold water over his head."

" It is very scrubby of you, Mark, to tell tales out of school," remonstrates Jack, amid the general laughter.

" John Chinaman would rather run a dozen miles than meet Jack when he was in one of his impulsive moods. He does not call it being in a temper, or a rage, or a passion, but merely being a *little impulsive*."

" That is worth remembering," says Mr. Dods ; " the next time I am reproached with scolding the congregation for bad attendance at the kirk, I shall say I am only following my impulses."

" Now, Miss Thyrza," calls Mark, " I believe it is left to you to give the *coup de grâce* and end our miseries."

Thyrza steps forward, and the balls being placed near the winning-post, puts them out one after another.

The victorious side wave their mallets over their heads in triumph.

" Well, Miss Jane, you deserved to win, for I think I only went through about six hoops," owns Mr. Lefroy, frankly.

" You did not require to tell me," returns

Jane, appeased by having won, " for I saw very well what was going on."

" Will you have your revenge?" asks Ferrier. " I daresay you will play the second game better and will be more used to the ground and the mallets."

CHAPTER IX.

IT is a wet day, in fact, a very wet day.
Wet days may be divided into two kinds,
those which make a feeble attempt at intervals
to clear up and often delude a pleasure party
into the mistaken belief that if they wait a little
longer it will soon be fine ; but this desirable
event does not happen, the sun remains behind
the cloud which perhaps has a " silver lining "
somewhere and the rain keeps on a gentle drizzle,
all the more irritating because it is just too
heavy to go out in, and has besides saturated the
grass and woods with wet. Then in opposition
to the undecided rainy day is the decided wet
day. This is more agreeable to deal with. One
knows what to do and what to expect; one is
not beguiled with delusive hopes of getting out;
and accepting fate quietly, one settles down to
one's work or letters with peacefulness. This is
unmistakeably a decided wet day. There is no

doubt about the way in which the rain pours down from the grey eaves, and trickles along the waterspouts. The weather has made up its mind to be wet, and wet it is. The wind howls mournfully round the house, and mixes with the racket of the waves on the rocks below as treble and bass mingle together in a duet.

Few visitors trouble Carmylie, even in fine weather; so on a day like this, of drenching rain, there is little chance of being disturbed by morning callers. Ferrier is in his study smoking a pipe and pondering over his father's debts, and a meeting he must shortly hold in Edinburgh with some of the Scotch creditors and his lawyers. His attitude is more easy than elegant, his feet resting on the top bar of the grate, in which burn pieces of peat and fir-wood, and his hands are crossed over his shoulders behind his neck. Dinner is in course of preparation in the kitchen. Cecilia is head cook besides being housekeeper, and some of her efforts would startle Mr. Lefroy. Her knowledge consists of how to make broth and boil beef, and she can also fry trout. That a little variation in the *menu* is desirable, never once occurs to her. On Jack's arrival from China, he had dismissed the cook and two housemaids, finding from a cursory glance at his father's papers that he could not afford to keep more servants than Rattray and Cecilia. Consequently, the household is rather primitive. The meals are served within half an hour or so of the time fixed, and it is Cecilia's opinion Mrs. Ferrier ought to be thankful to see dinner at all, instead of complaining that the roast hare is so peculiarly skewered it looks as if it were going to leap off the dish; or grumbling about the tea having been boiled before the fire until it is bitter as senna. Mrs. Napier's own maid, a supercilious woman—a bad imitation of her mistress in style and dress—is a thorn in the flesh to Cecilia.

Mrs. Ferrier has not been accustomed to housekeeping. Until latterly, she has always had a housekeeper. But, feeling for Jack, she has read up cookery books, and now ventures rather timidly into the kitchen to *beg* Cecilia to take pains with the stew.

Cecilia is not fond of being intruded upon in her own particular domain, " leddies should bide in their ain place, and she wad bide in hers." And after replying not very brightly, Mrs. Ferrier goes back to her sitting-room.

Rattray is making a " potato bogle," *Anglicè*, scarecrow, the day being too wet for him to do any outdoor work. He has got an old sack, an ancient hat, a ragged coat, and a quantity of sawdust, with which to stuff the figure.

Cecilia careers from pan to pan, lifting off lids and putting them on again, while Rattray whistles his favourite tune, " Charlie over the Water," and stitches the sack together with a darning needle and some twine.   He devises arms rather ingeniously by means of a piece of wood, and tying a string round the neck of the sack manufactures a round bullet-shaped knob intended for a head.

" Gae wa' oot o' that, Maister Davie !" exclaims Cecilia, " I'll no hae ye routing amang *my* pans.   Fat's that ye hae drappit into the watter butt at the door ? Gae wa' wi' ye."

" Would it not be jolly to paint eyes, nose, and mouth, on the bogle ?" says Davie, paying no heed to Cecilia, and abstracting a hot potato from one of the aforesaid pans, so hot that he dances in a sort of pantomime over the brick floor while peeling it.

" Fine," returns Rattray.   " But how would you pent them ?"

" You'll see," answers Davie, making a grab at Cecilia's cap in running out of the kitchen, and presently he comes back with a large camel's-hair paint brush, and a small bottle containing a dark fluid.

"That's no *pent*."

"Oh, isn't it? Just look how splendidly it takes it on."

"I dinna believe it's *pent*," persists Rattray, as Davie with a few touches of his brush produces a pair of goggle eyes, a nose a good deal to the one side, and a mouth literally from ear to ear.

"Will you let me paint *your* face, then?" asks Davie. "You can easily wash it off, you know."

"It's ower thin-like stuff for pent."

Davie does not wait for further permission, but dipping the brush into the dark fluid in the little bottle proceeds to paint whiskers on each side of Rattray's weatherbeaten cheeks among the stubble he carefully shaves off every Sunday morning.

"It has an awfu'-like *stink*," says Rattray, "will it be ink?"

"It's black paint, Rattray."

"I'm for nane upon my nose. It's a trick ye're up to, Davie."

"Oh, Rattray, just a little on the *tip* of your nose."

"I'm for nane o' your impidence! Ye are no kenning fat tae mak' o' yersel the day."

Davie throws the bottle away, and taking up

the coat stuffs the arms of the scarecrow into it. He is in the act of tying the hat on its head, when an exclamation from Rattray causes him to fly rapidly out at the kitchen door as if for his life, with Rattray at his heels.

"It's awfu' thochtless o' Henry tae leave the door that gait," says Cecilia, plaintively. "He'll hae the chimney on fire. Whiles there's nae comprehending thae men. Maybe he's gotten a flea in his ear."

"David, where is the key of mademoiselle's room?" calls Ferrier.

"He's awa' oot this blessed meenit, laird," returns Cecilia.

"Oh, laird, that laddie is needing his wheeps. He's gien me something that's taen the skin off my face."

"Where is the key of mademoiselle's room?" repeats Ferrier, sternly.

A voice replies "far up" the house from the top of a waterspout to which the culprit has scrambled with the agility of a squirrel, "*water-butt.*"

"Then, Rattray, you must fetch a ladder from the steading. Mademoiselle is locked in her room, and Davie has dropped the key in the butt. I have tried the keys of the other rooms and they won't fit the lock."

" Is he no tae get his wheeps, laird ?"

" Yes, if you can catch him," answers Ferrier, laughing at Rattray's indignation and the grimaces into which Davie, clinging on to the spout, is twisting his fair face.

While Rattray has gone for the ladder, Ferrier throws sundry tiny pebbles up to Thyrza's window.

" It will be all right directly," he says.

" Très bien, monsieur," rejoin treble accents from above.

" Hold the ladder steady, Rattray. Is this the longest you could find ?"

" Aweel, it is."

" What are those streaks you have on each cheek ?" he asks, ascending the ladder.

" I dinna ken, but they burn terrible. Davie pented the potato bogle first, and syne he's tae pent my face. He wanted tae pit some o' that black stuff on my nose, and it's a maircy I'd mair sense nor let him. I suspectit it was no vera richt when he mentioned the nose. I've wash'd them but they're nae better."

" I believe it's caustic, Rattray. It was lucky you were not such a soft as to let him do the whole of your face."

" Bide a wee till I catch ye, Maister David," shouts Rattray, holding the ladder with one hand

and shaking his closed fist in the direction of Davie.

Master Davie, although in rather a precarious situation, liberates one finger to place it in close proximity with a feature in his face which nature has not thought fit to render very prominent; indeed, it is a decided snub. However, snub noses have one decided advantage over those of a more classic type; they can be twisted from one side of the visage to the other, and are a great aid in the art of grimace making.

Ferrier reaches Thyrza's window and looks in.

" This is the only resource left, mademoiselle, unless you go up the chimney, as the door won't break open. Will it alarm you? I thought it would be easier if I came to guide you for the first few steps."

" No, monsieur."

" You had better not look down at the side of the house if you can help it."

" I always feel giddy on a high place."

" And yet you ran along the parapet of Bogg Bridge so carelessly. There was no sense in doing that. Now you want pluck you have none."

Thyrza climbs on to the sill by the assistance of a chair; Ferrier gives her his hand and holds her by the waist until her feet are firmly planted on the steps of the ladder.

"Now, do begin to move. It may be a romantic position this particularly *dry* day, but I don't relish it much." He is afraid for her up at such a great height, and has an uneasy recollection of noticing, as he ascended, that the ladder is rotten, or not very secure about the middle. But he dare not say anything for fear of rendering her more nervous.

"The losh keeps," exclaimed Rattray from below. "Are you and the laird tae bide a' day at the tap yonder?"

"I must let go, mademoiselle," pursues Ferrier.

"Oh, don't, monsieur."

"We shall never get down if I don't. Keep hold with both hands, and come cautiously, mademoiselle, thee's nowt but a *gawpin*, as they used to say at Marshley. What a fine view there is from here! There are splendid breakers on at the sand-bar. I could get a capital shot at that seagull if I had a gun."

Ferrier removes his hand from Thyrza's waist and goes down several steps, leaving her to come as she can.

"Courage, mademoiselle; if you fall you fall on me, and we shall both go together." Left to herself, Thyrza puts one foot and then the other down, and so arrives towards the bottom of the ladder, when it breaks in two and she only saves herself by springing to the ground.

" It is fortunate that did not happen before, or you and I should have damaged our necks a little I fear," says Jack, in his most frigid voice. " How came Davie to play such a trick as to lock you in? You are too young to have the care of such romping children."

" I don't know," answers Thyrza, recovered from her fright. " I went to make myself tidy, and when I wanted to get out the door was locked, and I screamed, and monsieur came and tried to break into the room, and he could not, and the keys did not fit, and *voilà tout*."

" *Tidy!*" rejoins Ferrier, with a queer look at Thyrza's hair, which *comme ordinaire* is in admired disorder, and the pin of her bow in the front of her gown has vanished, leaving it dangling ready to fall. " Next to a *sensible* woman I like to see a *tidy* one. Neatness is the sign of a well-balanced mind."

" I was under the impression I was very neat indeed," she returns, as they halt in the porch for a moment.

" Then I don't know what you *can* call *untidy!*"

" Ah, if you had seen me sometimes at the *pension* you would perceive one great improvement now."

"Well, I did not, and I am afraid I have lost something very valuable by not being there. May I venture to inquire how many hundred years you propose staying in this porch in a thorough draught?"

Meanwhile Rattray has picked up the broken ladder, and propping the longest end against the side of the house has scrambled up as far as he can go with safety. Davie crawls along the waterspout and stops short near Rattray. He is well aware nothing will be done to him. He has only to lie on his back and roar lustily to make both Mrs. Ferrier and Charity nearly go into hysterics. If old Mr. Ferrier had been alive Davie would not have ventured on such pranks, but even he had softened down a good deal before his death, and the mischief which would have been visited with condign punishment in his own sons merely drew a smile upon the grandchildren. As vexing or distressing Mrs. Ferrier in any way is the last thing Jack would do, Davie gets off scot free, although he considers he would be much benefited by an occasional thrashing. Davie approaches nearer Rattray.

The old man shakes his fist at him, and Davie adroitly slips on to a window-sill and seizes the ladder.

" Ye thrawn wratch !" cries Rattray, angrily,

" bide till I'm on the groond again and I'll gie ye it."

" Will you really?" says Davie, shaking the ladder violently.

" Oh, maircy, maircy !" exclaims Rattray.

" Will you promise not to say anything about it ?"

" Na, I'll promise naething."

" Then I'll shake the ladder until you fall," pursues Davie, knowing he has the best of it, and thoroughly enjoying Rattray's terror.

" Oh, oh ! I'll say naething mair, I winna, Maister Davie, I winna."

" Will you swear you won't ?" demanded the young rascal, giving the ladder a tremendous jerk.

" I'll sweer *onything, onything* ye like," pants Rattray, breathless with fear, willing to swear to whatever Davie wishes, and resolved to perjure himself the instant he touches *terra firma* again.

" Then I'll let you down," slackening his grasp of the ladder, on which it need hardly be said Rattray scuttles off it sideways, like a crab in a hurry, and ducks behind the water-butt. Davie, occupied with an acrobatic performance of sliding from the spout on to the ladder and descending at the gallop, is received almost into the very arms of Rattray, who has skulked out from his hiding-place. Davie, however, is slippery as an eel, and three times as supple as Rattray; he twists himself from his embrace by a somersault, regains his footing, and is in the house and upstairs with Mrs. Ferrier before Rattray has been able to rise from the wet dank grass.

"Are you busy, mademoiselle?" asks Ferrier, entering the schoolroom some few minutes later.

"Not very, monsieur."

"Could you spare me a few minutes?"

"Yes," says Thyrza, rather wonderingly, "I could, but I am not sure that I shall."

"Why not? What have I done to incur your displeasure?"

"You told me I was very untidy."

"So you were."

"But I am neat now, am I not?"

"Well," doubtfully, looking at the simple print gown and blue bow at the throat, which she has put on since coming out of her room by the ladder, having found it in the schoolroom, "it's *better*. But did you *ever* pin your collar *straight* in your life?"

"Is it not straight?"

"No; a quarter of an inch too much to the left. I have got a letter from my French agent which I can't quite make out. The idioms are so bothering and the fellow writes such an odd hand, otherwise I should not trouble you."

" It will be no trouble. I suppose monsieur desires that I should translate it into English for him ?"

" Exactly so."

" Shall I begin now ? Where is the letter ?"

" It is in my study. I think you will find it easier to write a translation of it there, especially as there are a number of trade terms in it which without me you would be unable to understand. Will you come then ?"

Ferrier's study is the morning-room which belonged to the late Mr. Ferrier. It is fitted up with light oak and dark blue hangings powdered with gold fleur-de-lis, with carpet and furniture to match, of blue and oak. Pictures on the walls of racehorses in almost every possible attitude, reveal the taste uppermost in the mind of the previous owner. On a writing-desk is an inkstand composed of four horse-hoofs set in silver, formerly appertaining to a favourite mare of Mr. Ferrier's. Round the room are hung a collection of antique pistols and guns and fowling-pieces, and some magnificent trophies of big game, sent home from India by Captain Napier ; heads of tigers and elks and antelopes, and the striped skin that once covered the treacherous, cruel form of a huge man-eater now serves the peaceful purpose of a comfortable hearthrug. On a table strewn with papers, blue envelopes, and ledgers, are several morocco-cases of jewels belonging to Mrs. Ferrier. They are to be sold by her own wish, and contain trinkets of great value.

"There is a seat, mademoiselle," says Ferrier, dragging out a large arm-chair for her. Thyrza sits down and translates the small, elaborate writing of the Frenchman into English.

"Koonfongs?" she asks, inquiringly. "And No. 1 and No. 2 tsatlee koonfongs, Hs?"

"Oh, merely trade terms. Stick to the point in question. What is it the man wants to say about seeing me in the autumn. Does he want me to go, or does he not?"

"I have not finished yet, but I shall in another moment. Shall I write it out for you, or read it aloud?"

"Write it out, please, and then I shall not forget it."

She copies out the translation and hands it to Ferrier. After he has read it through, he apparently waits for her to abandon her seat and leave the room.

"Can I help monsieur?" she says, when

Ferrier has been so good as to remark he considers the translation "not bad."

"You have already done so. I think there is nothing more in the way of further assistance that you can do. You cannot add up the accounts; I suspect your arithmetic is of an Irish nature—Twice five is six; the nines in four you *can't*, so dot three and carry one, and let the rest walk !"

"Oh no," returns Thyrza, earnestly, "indeed it is not. And I do want to let you see that I am *not* silly and foolish."

"If you imagine I think you are so, you must know my thoughts better than I know them myself."

"But you said I was silly."

"You are not more foolish than most girls, and a great deal wiser than some," he rejoins, a little impatiently, "but you must not mind what *I* say. I don't know much about girls. During the past few years, as I have already told you, I have seen precious few specimens, and I must own what I have seen did not make me wish to see any more," laying down his pen, and strangling a violent yawn that is trying hard to get into existence.

"I *do* mind what you say. I can't bear for

you to think me a *simpering nothing.* I want you to believe I am not stupid."

" I don't say you are a simpering young woman. Far from it."

This comes of being out of the ordinary run. No good ever results from that. Well, she is no relation of his, so it does not signify.

" But I can't believe you are wise when you are *not*," he goes on very distinctly, " no young persons are. When you are older and have seen the world you will have acquired knowledge, and have learnt how to use the common sense with which nature has provided you———"

" I wish I was old," she bursts forth, impetuously.

" Time will soon cure that fault. What is the matter ?"

" Oh, nothing," she says, abruptly, turning away.

" Well, then ; I will swear you are wiser than Solomon."

" No, *don't*, I had much rather you said what you thought. I should *hate* for you to say untruths only to *please* me, as if I were a *baby*."

" *Hate !* is not that rather strong language considering the occasion ? There is no pleasing you. If I say what I think, you are—impul-

sive; if I flatter you, it is worse. What shall
I do?"

"I don't want to be flattered or compli-
mented; if monsieur would let me assist him,"
she rejoins, persuasively, "I used to copy out
Mr. Spindler's musical compositions for him,
and I never made any mistakes. Besides, there
is no fear of——" pausing.

"Of what? Go on, mademoiselle."

"There is no fear of you falling in love with
me," says she quietly, without an atom of co-
quettishness in her manner.

"Speak for yourself," returns Ferrier, gravely,
"how do you know that?"

"Because you told me so."

"Do you believe everything you are told?
You ought to believe *nothing* of what you hear,
and only a quarter of what you see. What's
the use of my thinking well of you? It won't
do you any *good,* or make you a bit the *happier,*
or put any *money* into your pocket."

"Monsieur is so clever; his opinion is worth
having."

"I am afraid I am only a poor devil at the
best, a man of no account," and Ferrier gives
a little sigh; "it is really very amiable of you
to wish to help me, but I scarcely think you
understand what you want to undertake. Shall

I instal you in office as my clerk? 'Yes,' you answer, but I shall perhaps be cross and scold; then the tide will come in and you will cry."

"Oh no," she replied, with a bright smile, "I never cry. I am sure I should not."

"Well, I will tell you what I am about. You may have heard that I am rich, but in fact I am poor as a church mouse. These books here are the lawyers' accounts which I am looking over. Now, you don't know the difference between single and double entry."

"Well, it is a fact I do not, but I can learn," says she with another smile, which makes Ferrier inwardly determine he will not invite this new kind of clerk to return to his study, otherwise the play will end in a word of four letters—Love.

"You would learn Chinese as quickly," he answered, gruffly; "however, I will give you a trial. First of all, seven times eight?"

" Fifty-six."

" Are you certain?"

" Sans doute, monsieur."

" Nine times nine?"

" Eighty-one."

" Once one?"

" Two."

Ferrier shakes his head.

"Won't do."

" Ah, what stupid I am!   One of course."

" So far, so good.   Please give me your undivided attention.   There are the leases of the grass *parks*—Scotch term that for meadows—at Carmylie for the last eight years, add up the sum total, and as you wish to be useful, will you sew a button on this wristband for me?   Needle and thread are just at hand in Charity's workbox."

Whether nervous or not cannot precisely be said, but Thyrza bungles in threading her needle, and only after an attempt of about a minute, does she discover that the reason of her non-success lies in the eye being filled up.   Even then, she does not thread it with her usual quickness.   However, this being finished, she turns to Ferrier.

" As you are so kind, mademoiselle, this is where the deficiency lies."

She bends down to stitch on the button, unconscious of the quickening of Ferrier's pulse, like electric wildfire, as her brown soft fingers accidentally touch his strong muscular wrist, and a tress of her flowing locks rests for an instant on his dark bronzed cheek.   She is so close to him that he can almost hear her heart beating rapidly under its thin print covering.   Intent on her work, she does not notice the glance he fixes upon her.

" It is not now properly sewn on. See what a little thing is sufficient to break it off," he exclaims, treacherously wrenching it off, in order to have the pleasure of Thyrza sewing it on again. " Your education has evidently been neglected. Before trying to be a clerk, you should get up thoroughly the arts belonging to your own sex. Seventeen years of age, and not able to stitch on a button."

" It is monsieur's fault, and monsieur has no manners," remonstrates Thyrza, threading her needle once again, and beginning her task once more in all innocence, " if monsieur would remain tranquil I could do it very well."

"Ah, you've pricked your finger ; poor little brown finger."

" Don't pity me," says she, viciously.

" You should not undertake more than you can do."

She gives a little stamp and snaps the thread.

" Sew it on yourself," she exclaims, and throwing the needle into the fire, she moves towards the door preparing to make her exit, when Jack prevents her by standing with his back set against the panels.

" We should never have got on as master

and clerk. Nature knew a long way the best when she made you a woman, but that sensitive disposition of yours so touchy—— "

" I am not touchy."

" I beg your pardon, you *are* touchy. That disposition would have got you into dreadful scrapes as a man. Why, you would have been knocking down every second fellow you met, because he happened to say something which offended you. Look here, mademoiselle, I want you to make friends with Charity. You will learn from her those nice feminine ways which are so taking."

" I can't endure nice feminine ways," protests Thyrza, thoroughly provoked. " Why should not a man and woman be able to be friends without falling in love ?"

" Not a very relevant question," returns Ferrier, in an exasperatingly cool tone of voice, still keeping his back firmly pressed against the door. " Because any experiment of the kind I ever heard of has been a failure."

" Monsieur, I wish to return to my school-room ; please open the door."

" Pardon me, you have not fulfilled your part of the bargain," says he ; " I believe you promised to help me about the grass leases."

" Well !"

"I will explain it to you if you will attend. There are so many fields—you will find the number on referring to the papers—each containing so many acres of land let at so much per pole, and varying in price as the land varies in value. It is as easy as A B C."

But Thyrza is too much offended to be at once consoled and appeased. Ferrier quits the door. He comes to her. Her left hand—the forefinger of which was wounded in his service—hangs limply down, and on the said small forefinger there is a little red stain.

"I never thought monsieur could have laughed at me," she answers, in return to his expressions of penitence, rubbing off the stain with her handkerchief.

"I am too old and stiff to go down on my knees, mademoiselle, or I would do so and apologize," he entreats.

Thyrza yields at his contrition and believes that had he not been in truth too stiff, he would have sued forgiveness from his bended knees, and she takes up her position at the table.

Arithmetic, unfortunately, is her weak point. She cannot add up or divide the smallest sum mentally, and even if provided with pencil and paper before her she still requires some length of time for reflection. The famous "herring and

a half" has only been solved by her during the
past year, and though clever enough in other
departments, she could never have gained a prize
in the mathematical line. I am afraid she would
have been plucked in an examination at Oxford
or Cambridge. Her imaginative powers are
much greater than her arithmetical abilities. One
reason for this may be that arithmetic, beyond
the four simple rules, has never been clearly explained to her. Now, she is excited, and without
pausing to think goes to work at once, sets down
the number of acres carefully and the price
which they fetched during one grazing season.
Ferrier has told her to ascertain the amount
which the lot will come to for each year sepa-
rately. This is because in some seasons the
fields realized more than at others. And then
having found the sum for each year to add the
produce of the eight years together. This, of
course, would give the sum total. But Thyrza,
in her haste to do it well and fast, forgets the
simple directions, and is presently involved in
calculations between cyphers and an odd process
of counting which would have made the hair
of any good arithmetician stand on end. Then
she cannot remember for her very existence how
many poles there are in an acre, and she is too
proud to ask.

Ferrier, meanwhile, transcribes quickly into a large book, and then answers a letter from ·his lawyer in Edinburgh. He writes a small, clear, business-like hand. There is a good deal of character in the decisive, steady letters, formed without a tremor or falter. He reads over the epistle before closing it for the purpose of discovering whether any words have been left out; then he seals the envelope with his crest. It is also like the man that the seal is well done and perfectly impressed—not an indistinct line in the largely-engraved crest. When this is finished he looks at Thyrza. She is struggling with the sum, which being worked in the wrong way shows an aggregate of several thousand pounds. She bites her lips and wrinkles her blue-veined forehead into deep frowns. She grows hot and pushes her troublesome hair away from her shoulders. As she is doing the sum with pen and ink, she cannot rub out the working. One or two sheets of paper she covers with figures and blots, which are as fast destroyed. Ferrier rises and leans over the back of her chair to examine the progress of the sum. She bows down her head and stretches her hands over the last sheet.

"Let me look," he says.

"I shan't," she rejoins, raising her head and

doubling up the paper. Ferrier lays his hand on it. She tears it into little bits; but she is not so quick about it that Ferrier has not contrived to catch a glimpse of the total result.

"Three thousand five hundred pounds for the rent of about a dozen and a half of fields from Whitsuntide to Martinmas. By Jove, I wish I had you for a tenant. Matters would soon square themselves at that rate. How many poles are there in an acre?"

"I—don't—know," very slowly, and passing an inky finger over her cheek, she leaves thereon a smudge.

"I think there are something like forty and a quarter. Are you vexed, mademoiselle?"

"No-o-o," doubtfully and prolonged.

"You forgot what I told you. By-the-bye, you've inked your face."

"Have I?"

"You want a looking-glass, I see. There is not one in this room. You are only making it worse. Stay, I daresay you can manage with this," pulling out his watch and opening it where it is wound up. "When I've been badly off I've often put my tie straight by its means."

Thyrza takes the watch and removes the smudge, Ferrier contemplating her the while.

"The most beautiful looking-glass I ever saw is here just now," he says, presently.

"Where, monsieur?" she inquires, regarding him steadfastly.

"In your eyes," he answered. "I seem a different man when I look at myself in them."

"In *my eyes*, monsieur?"

"Yes, in your eyes. If you look into mine you will see yourself reflected, very small, it is true, but quite perfect. Tell me what you see now?"

"Well, it is a fact," she exclaims, joyfully; "I do really see myself, monsieur."

"I see in *your* eyes the reflection of a man, who *might* have been much better, and a respectable fellow, but who instead went all wrong, and is now getting content to drift where fate drives him."

"Then you don't see yourself, monsieur. How is it that I saw myself so well?"

"There is a *great* difference between your eyes and mine."

"Is there? But how? And who is it you saw?"

"I can't explain the difference between our eyes, so well as I can this sum about the grass leases. Eighteen hundred and sixty-four seems to have been a capital year for the parks. How many are there ? Fifteen ; I suppose some land must have been reclaimed from the heather, as afterwards they increase to eighteen and nineteen."

He sits down beside Thyrza, taking a fresh sheet of paper, and setting the sum in clear neat figures, does it for her, explaining the reason of each mode of working. After this, he destroys it and makes Thyrza go through the whole herself, figure by figure, and refuses to assist her when her memory failing her for a moment, she forgets what she ought to do next. Then after she has finished the whole triumphantly, and copied it tidily into one of the large ledgers she rises, crying delightedly—

"Now, monsieur, allow that I am of some use."

"I don't know how it strikes you, but it strikes me that calculating the time, the waste of paper and ink, &c., I might almost as well have done it myself," returns Ferrier, drily.

Thyrza walks right out of the room, banging the door after her, as an outlet to her feelings. It is amazing how refreshing a little explosion of the kind is when one is slightly agitated.

"Mademoiselle, mademoiselle," shouts Ferrier, "as we live under the same roof-tree, let us be at peace. Will not you excuse my—impulsiveness, and stitch on that shirt-button ?"

" That I never will," returns Thyrza, hotly. " And I'll never come back to your study, never, and you may translate your letters as you can."

" A regular little pepper-pot," reflects Ferrier, returning to his peculiar sanctum, and lighting a cigar, " she's quite right about keeping out of this study. If she came often I should be making a fool of myself. It's better we should be at daggers drawn. Jove! I was very near giving her a kiss, and I believe I should if I had not cut up deuced nasty that minute. She'll think me a brute. Hang those infernal debts, I shall never get rid of them all my life. I wish Charity had engaged a woman of an awkward age."

" Please, sir; the meenister has called tae speir for ye," says Cecilia, sticking her head into the study.

" Tell the minister I am not at home," answers Ferrier, promptly; going to the open window, from which he beholds Mr. Dods in his Sunday-go-to-meeting broadcloth, waiting under an umbrella on the gravel sweep.

The almost instantaneous result of this reply is the following, delivered in Cecilia's squeakiest tones—

" The laird is i' the hoose, but he's no at home."

"In the house, but not at home?" repeated the minister. "De-ar me!"

"I dinna ken nae mair," pursues Cecilia, "that's a' the laird tellt me tae tell ye, and I hae tellt ye exack."

The minister retires down the brae to the fishing village.

END OF VOL. I.